Buffy the Vampire Slayer™

Autumnal

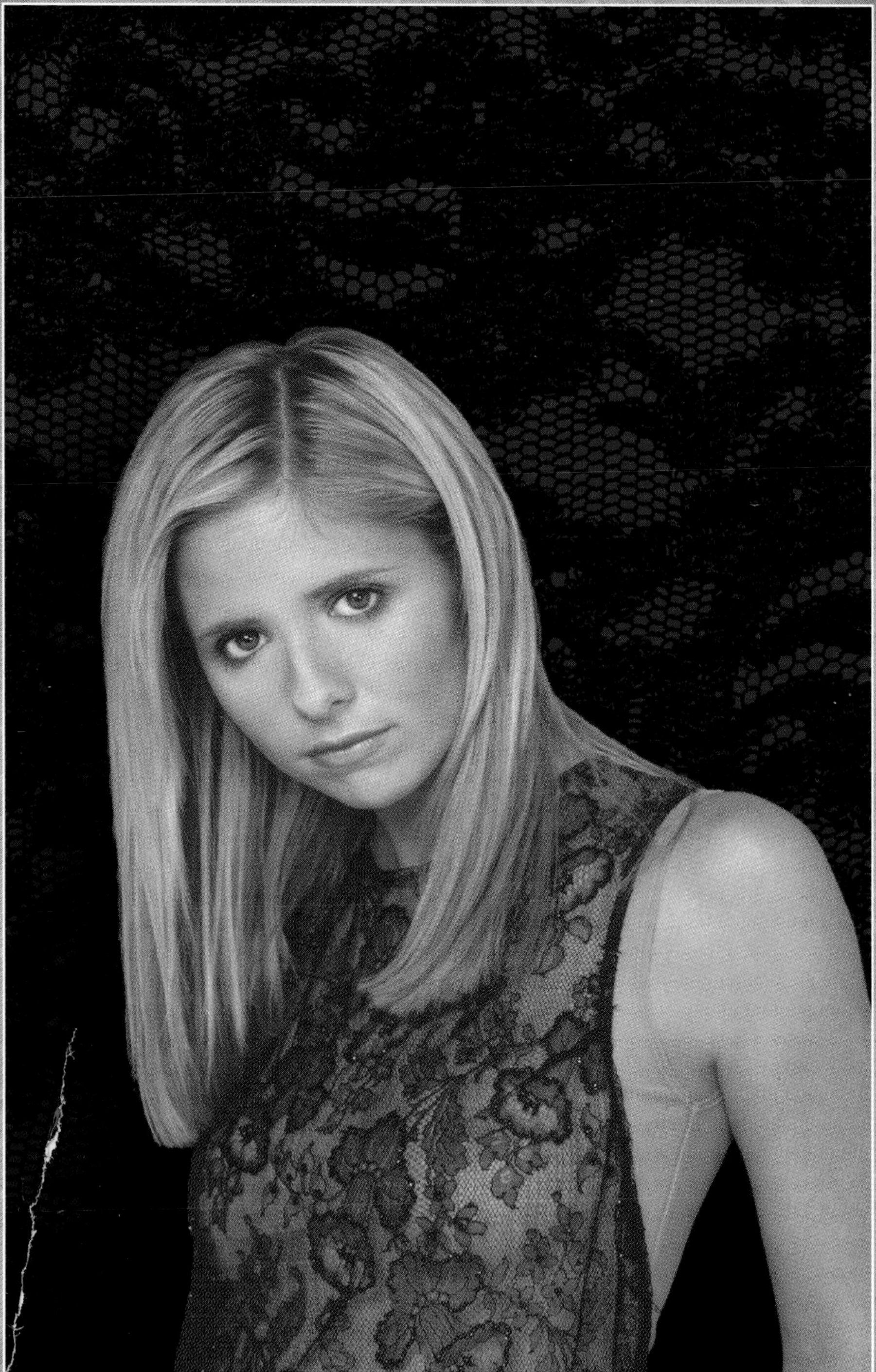

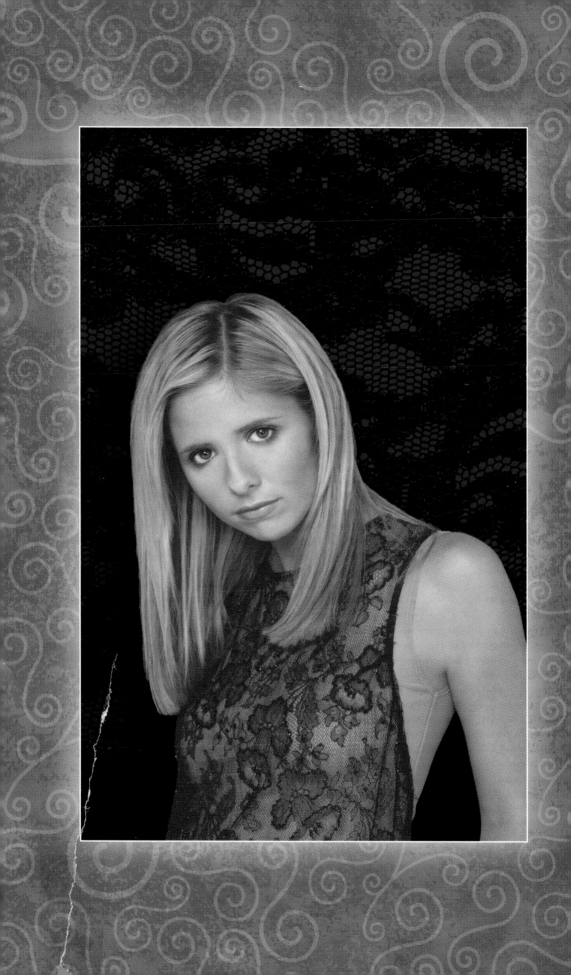

Buffy the Vampire Slayer

AUTUMNAL

based on the television series created by
JOSS WHEDON

"The Heart of a Slayer" written by **CHRIS BOAL**

"The Cemetery of Lost Love" written by **TOM FASSBENDER & JIM PASCOE**

penciller **CLIFF RICHARDS**

inker **JOE PIMENTEL**

colorist **GUY MAJOR**

letterer **CLEM ROBINS**

These stories take place during Buffy the Vampire Slayer's fourth season.

dark horse comics®

publisher
MIKE RICHARDSON

editor
SCOTT ALLIE
with ADAM GALLARDO *and* MICHAEL CARRIGLITTO

collection designers
KEITH WOOD *and* DARCY HOCKETT

art director
MARK COX

special thanks to
DEBBIE OLSHAN AT FOX LICENSING,
CAROLINE KALLAS AND GEORGE SNYDER AT *BUFFY THE VAMPIRE SLAYER*,

Buffy the Vampire Slayer™: Autumnal. Published by Dark Horse Comics, Inc., 10956 SE Main Street, Milwaukie, OR, 97222.
Buffy the Vampire Slayer™ & © 2001 Twentieth Century Fox Film Corporation. All rights reserved.
TM designates a trademark of Twentieth Century Fox Film Corporation. The stories, institutions, and characters in this publication are fictional.
Any resemblance to actual persons, living or dead, events, institutions, or locales, without satiric intent, is purely coincidental.
No portion of this book may be reproduced, by any means, without express written permission from
the copyright holder. Dark Horse Comics® and the Dark Horse logo are trademarks of Dark Horse Comics, Inc.,
registered in various categories and countries. All rights reserved.

PUBLISHED BY
DARK HORSE COMICS, INC.
10956 SE MAIN STREET
MILWAUKIE, OR 97222

FIRST EDITION
OCTOBER 2001
ISBN: 1 - 56971 - 554 - 8

1 3 5 7 9 10 8 6 4 2

printed in singapore.

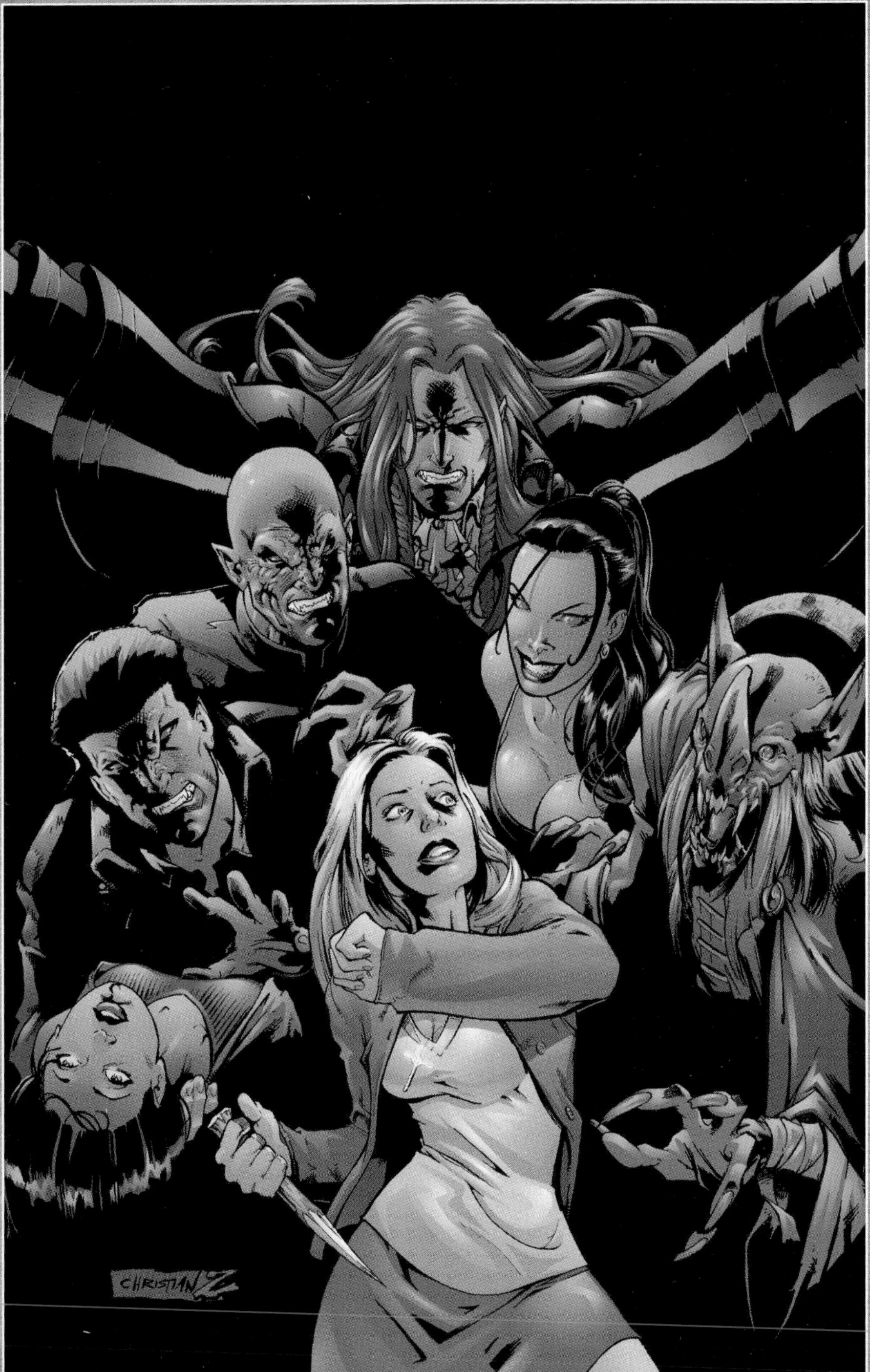
CHRISTIAN Z

Art by CHRISTIAN ZANIER
with DAVE STEWART

THE HEART OF A SLAYER

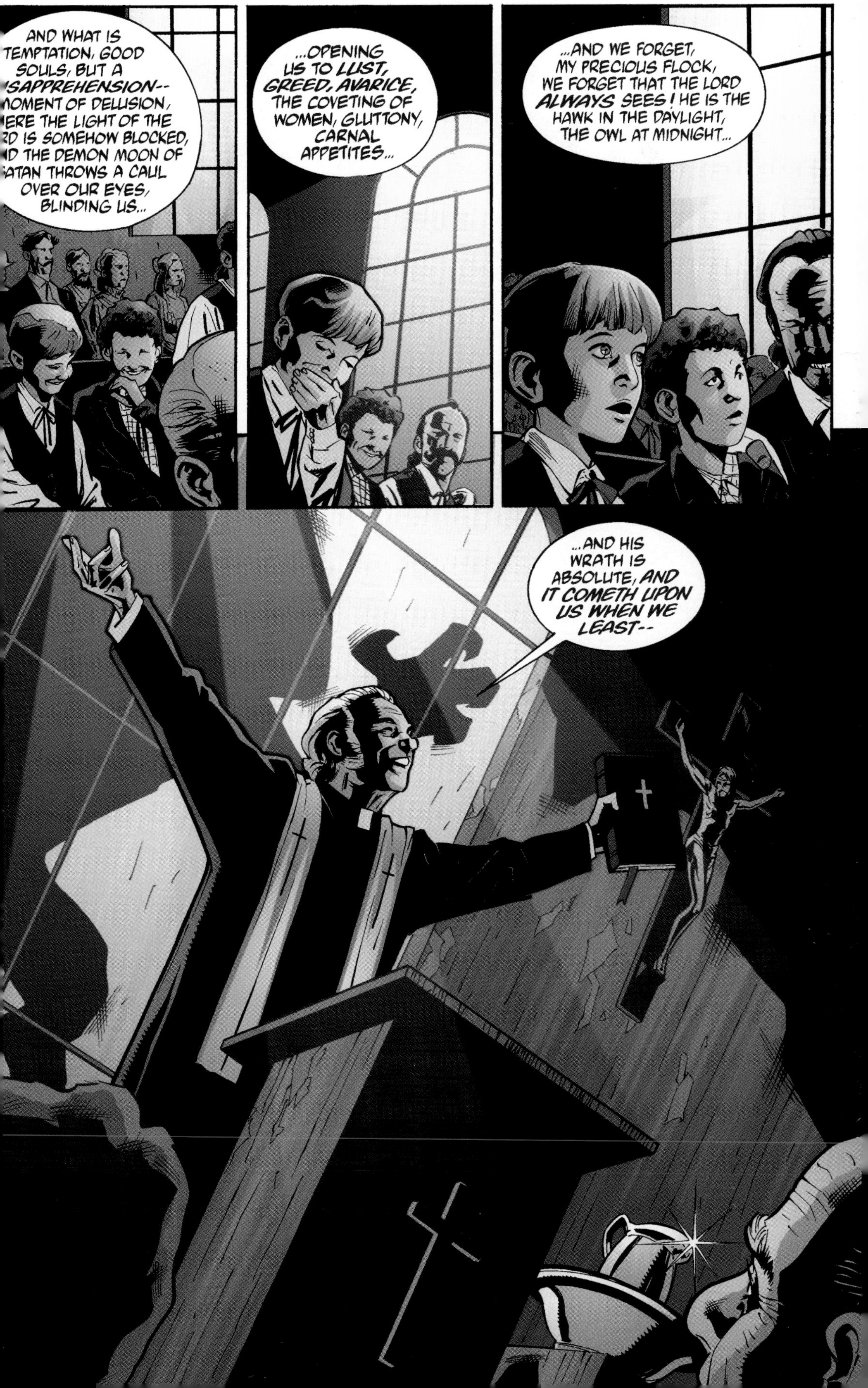
AND WHAT IS TEMPTATION, GOOD SOULS, BUT A ISAPPREHENSION-- MOMENT OF DELUSION, HERE THE LIGHT OF THE D IS SOMEHOW BLOCKED, D THE DEMON MOON OF ATAN THROWS A CAUL OVER OUR EYES, BLINDING US...
...OPENING US TO LUST, GREED, AVARICE, THE COVETING OF WOMEN, GLUTTONY, CARNAL APPETITES...
...AND WE FORGET, MY PRECIOUS FLOCK, WE FORGET THAT THE LORD ALWAYS SEES! HE IS THE HAWK IN THE DAYLIGHT, THE OWL AT MIDNIGHT...
...AND HIS WRATH IS ABSOLUTE, AND IT COMETH UPON US WHEN WE LEAST--

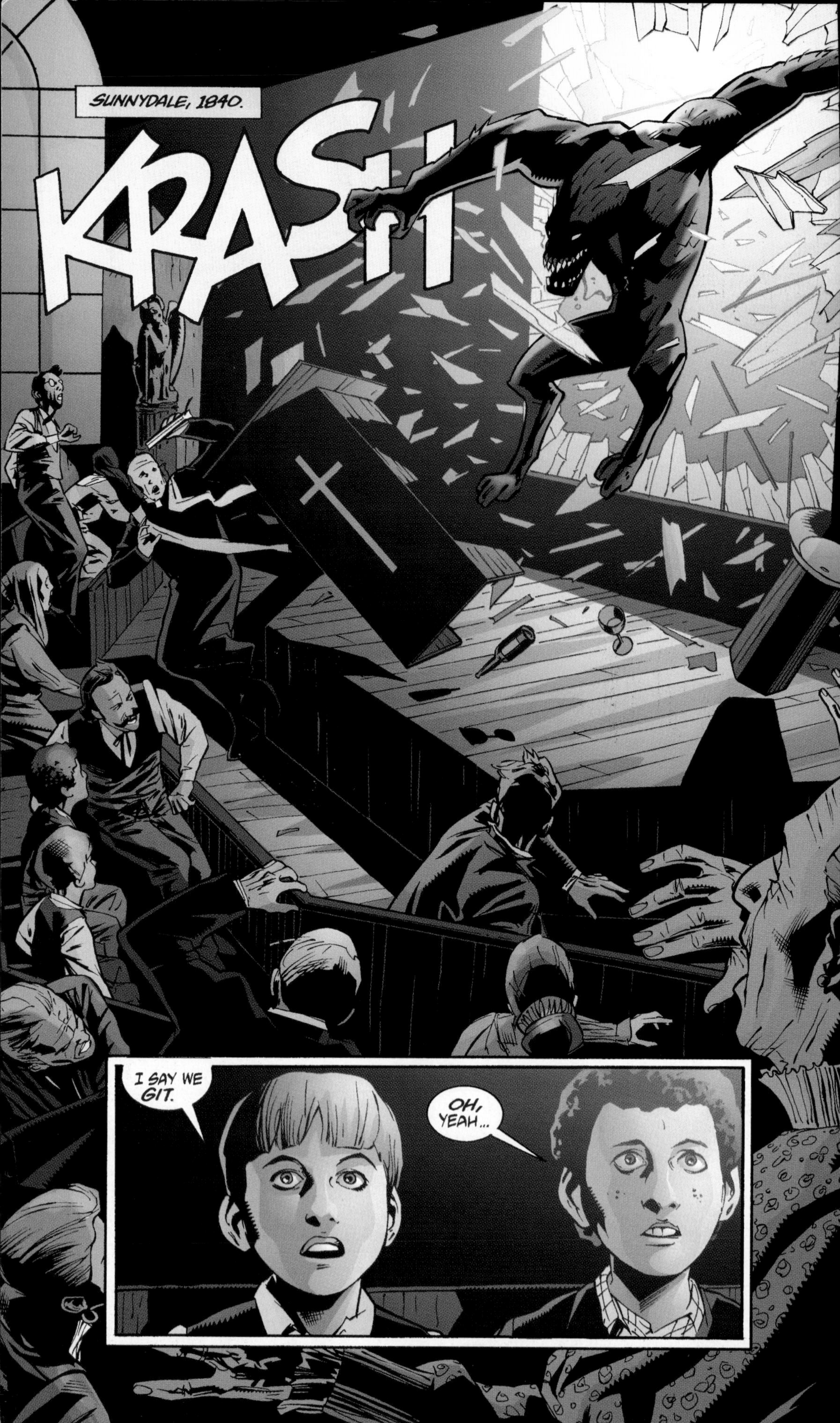
SUNNYDALE, 1840.
KRASH
I SAY WE GIT.
OH, YEAH...

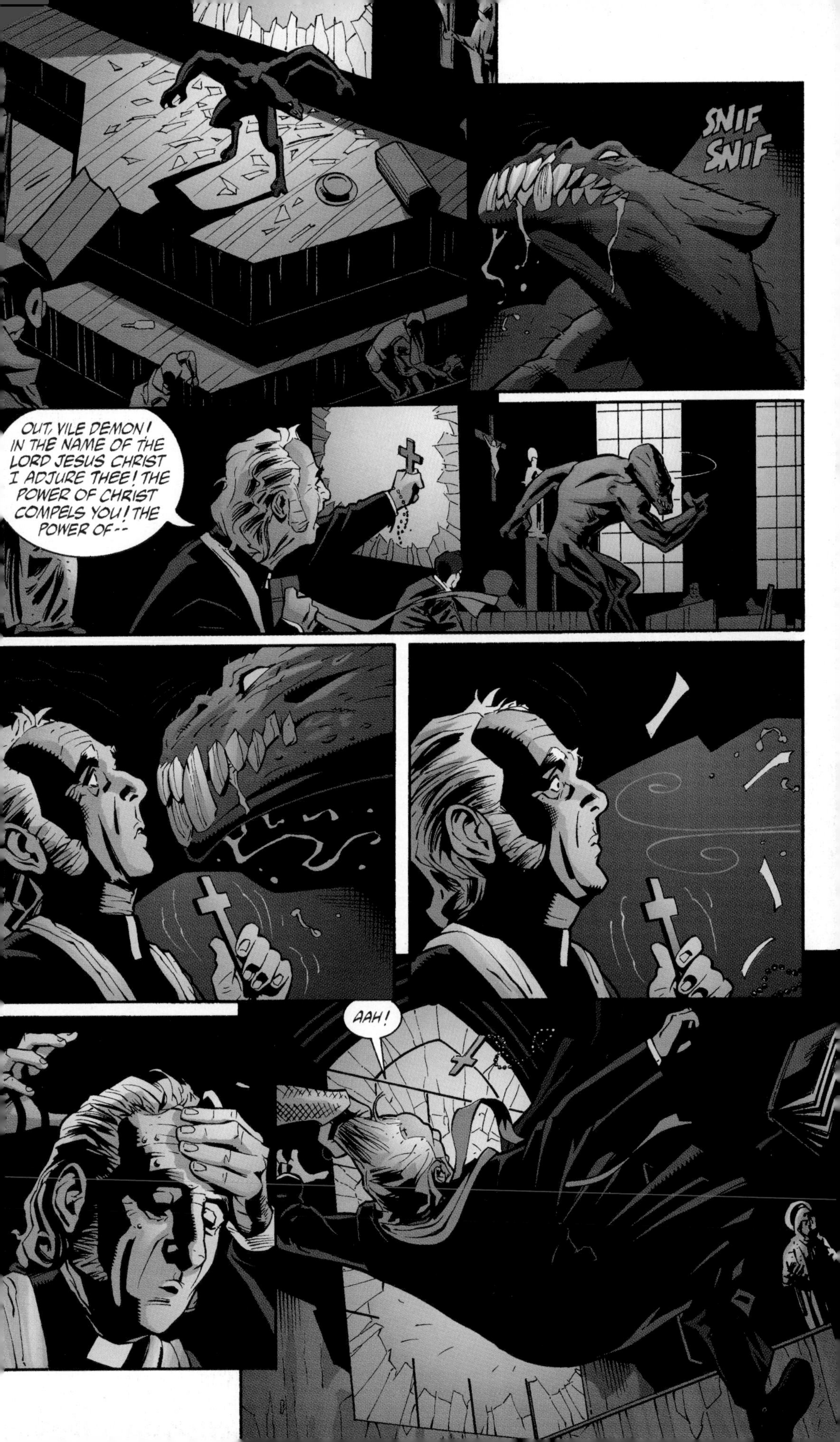
SNIF
SNIF
OUT, VILE DEMON! IN THE NAME OF THE LORD JESUS CHRIST I ADJURE THEE! THE POWER OF CHRIST COMPELS YOU! THE POWER OF--
AAH!

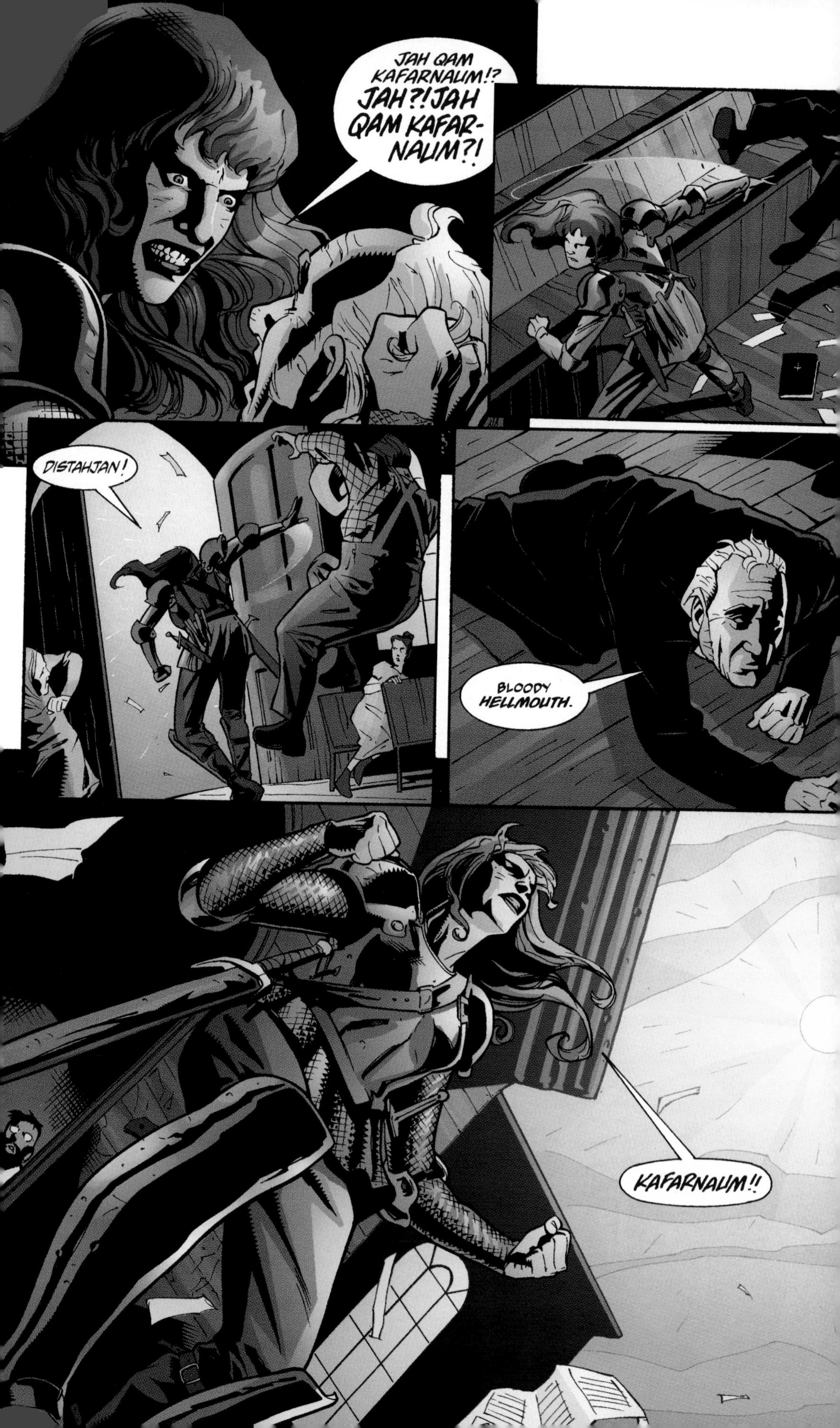
JAH QAM KAFARNAUM!? JAH?! JAH QAM KAFARNAUM?!
DISTAHJAN!
BLOODY HELLMOUTH.
KAFARNAUM!!

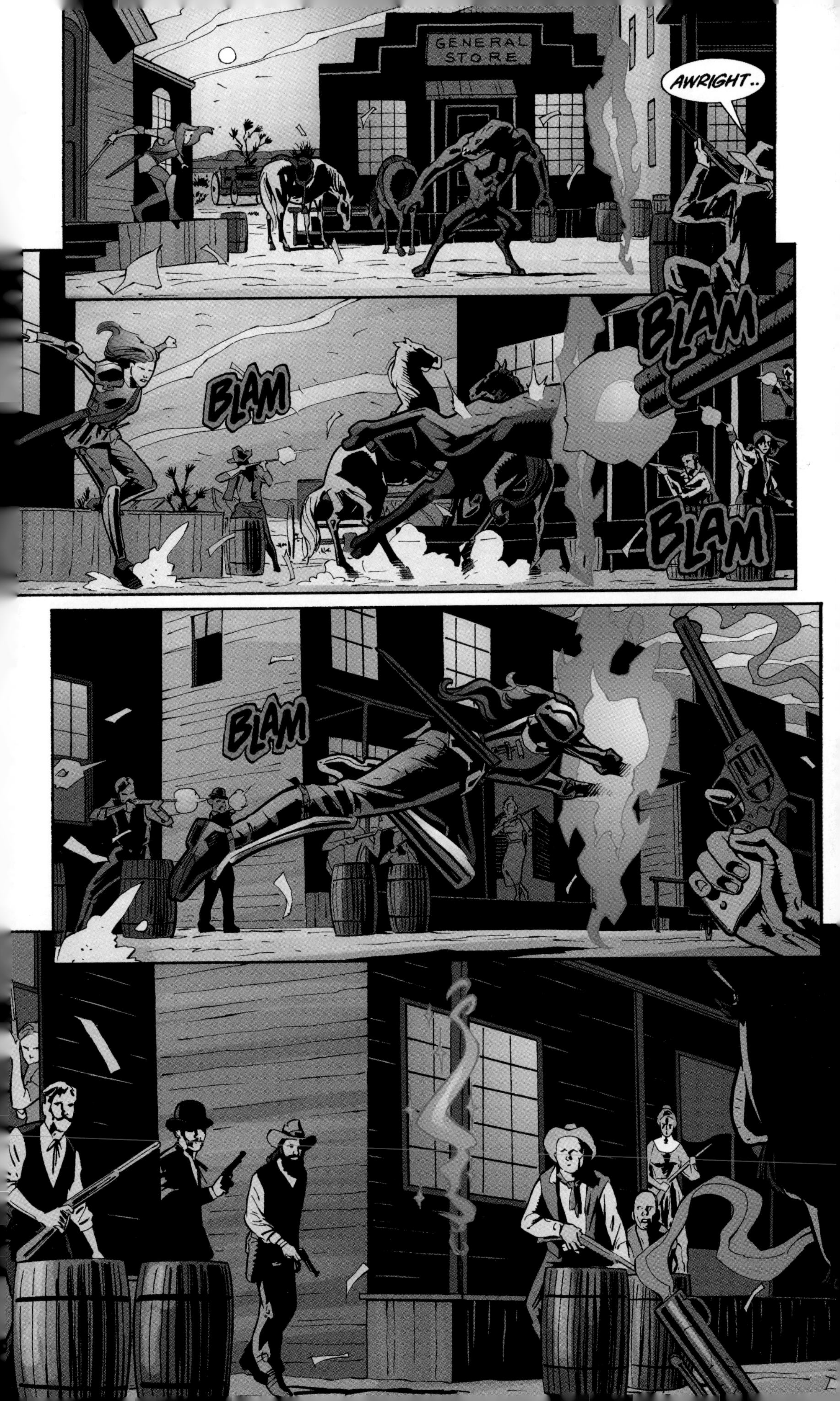
GENERAL STORE
AWRIGHT..
BLAM
BLAM
BLAM
BLAM

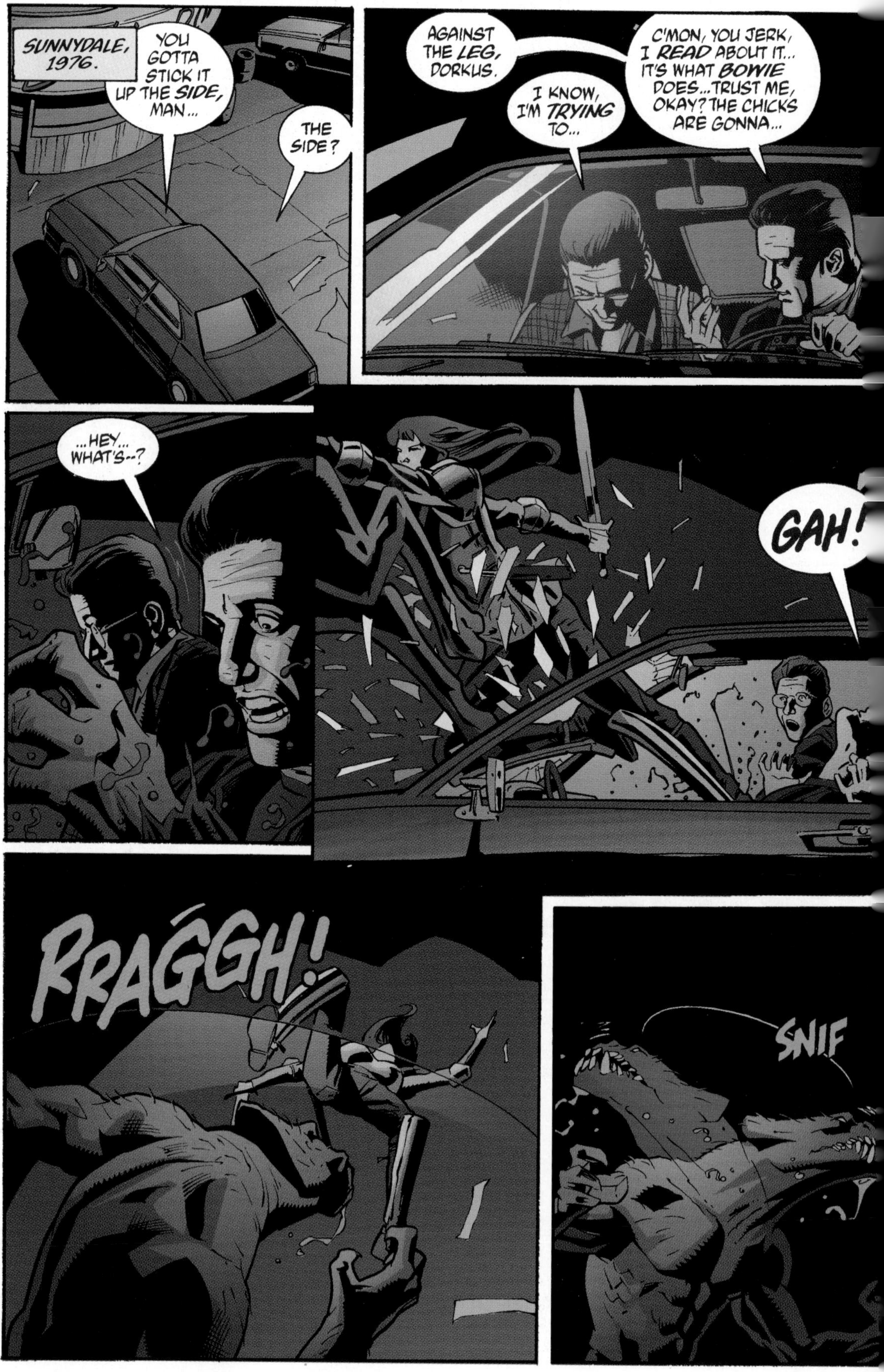
SUNNYDALE, 1976.
YOU GOTTA STICK IT UP THE SIDE, MAN...
THE SIDE?
AGAINST THE LEG, DORKUS.
I KNOW, I'M TRYING TO...
C'MON, YOU JERK, I READ ABOUT IT... IT'S WHAT BOWIE DOES...TRUST ME, OKAY? THE CHICKS ARE GONNA...
...HEY... WHAT'S--?
GAH!
RRAGGH!
SNIF

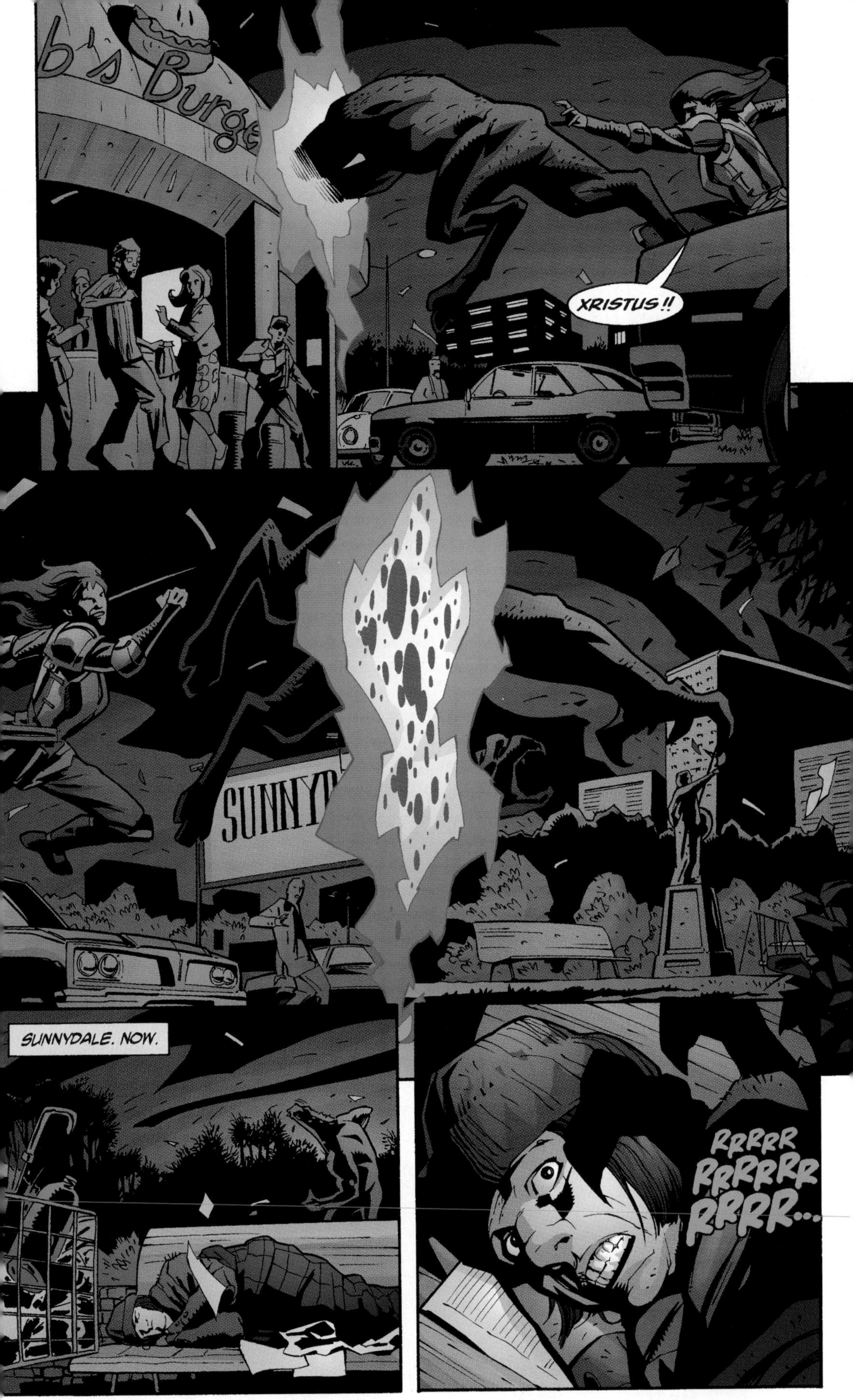

b's Burge
XRISTUS!!
SUNNY
SUNNYDALE. NOW.
RRRRR RRRRRR RRRR...

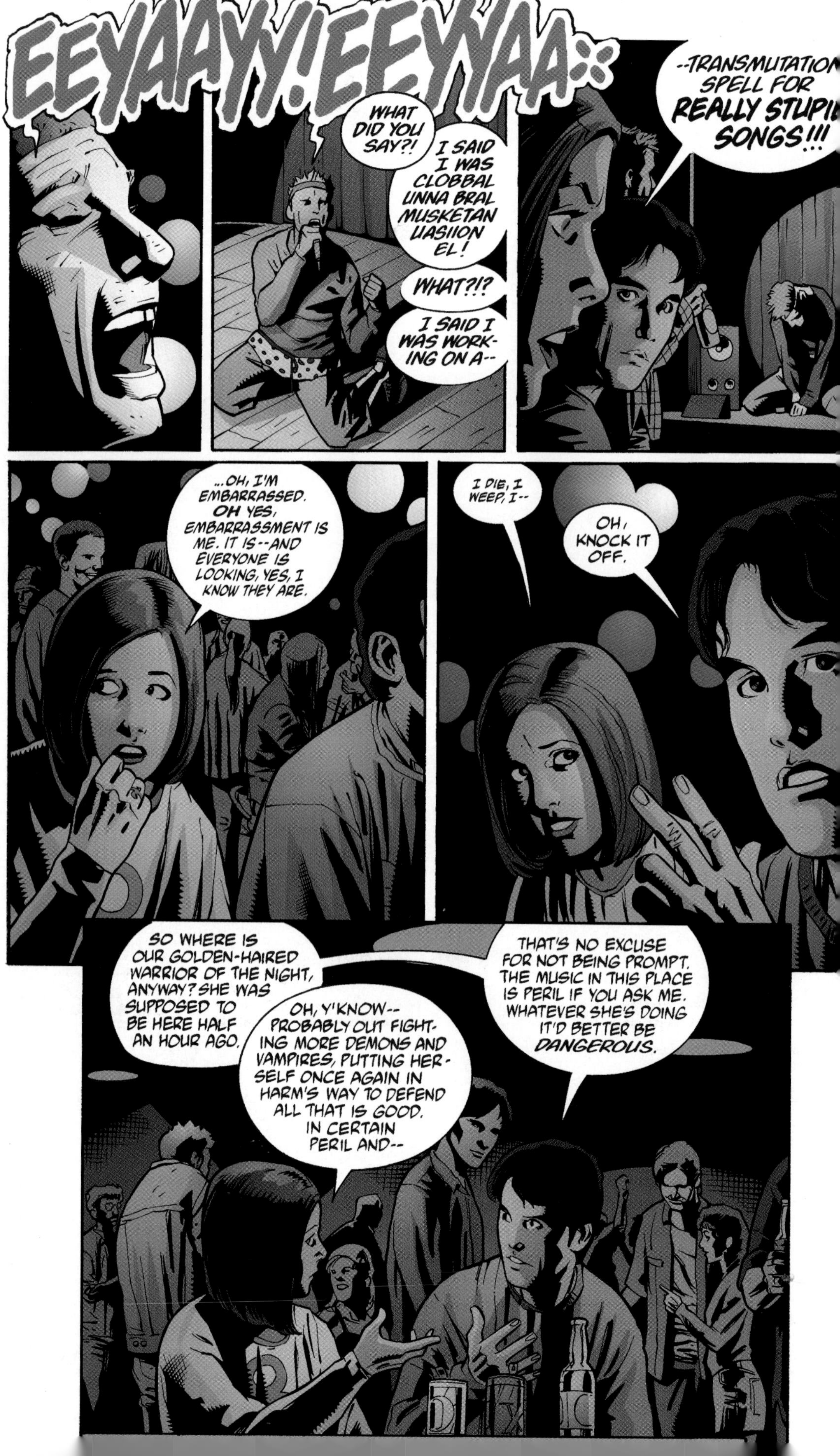

EEYAAYY! EEYYAA::
WHAT DID YOU SAY?!
I SAID I WAS CLOBBAL UNNA BRAL MUSKETAN UASIION EL!
WHAT?!?
I SAID I WAS WORKING ON A--
--TRANSMUTATION SPELL FOR REALLY STUPI SONGS!!!
...OH, I'M EMBARRASSED. OH YES, EMBARRASSMENT IS ME. IT IS--AND EVERYONE IS LOOKING, YES, I KNOW THEY ARE.
I DIE, I WEEP, I--
OH, KNOCK IT OFF.
SO WHERE IS OUR GOLDEN-HAIRED WARRIOR OF THE NIGHT, ANYWAY? SHE WAS SUPPOSED TO BE HERE HALF AN HOUR AGO.
OH, Y'KNOW-- PROBABLY OUT FIGHTING MORE DEMONS AND VAMPIRES, PUTTING HERSELF ONCE AGAIN IN HARM'S WAY TO DEFEND ALL THAT IS GOOD. IN CERTAIN PERIL AND--
THAT'S NO EXCUSE FOR NOT BEING PROMPT. THE MUSIC IN THIS PLACE IS PERIL IF YOU ASK ME. WHATEVER SHE'S DOING IT'D BETTER BE DANGEROUS.

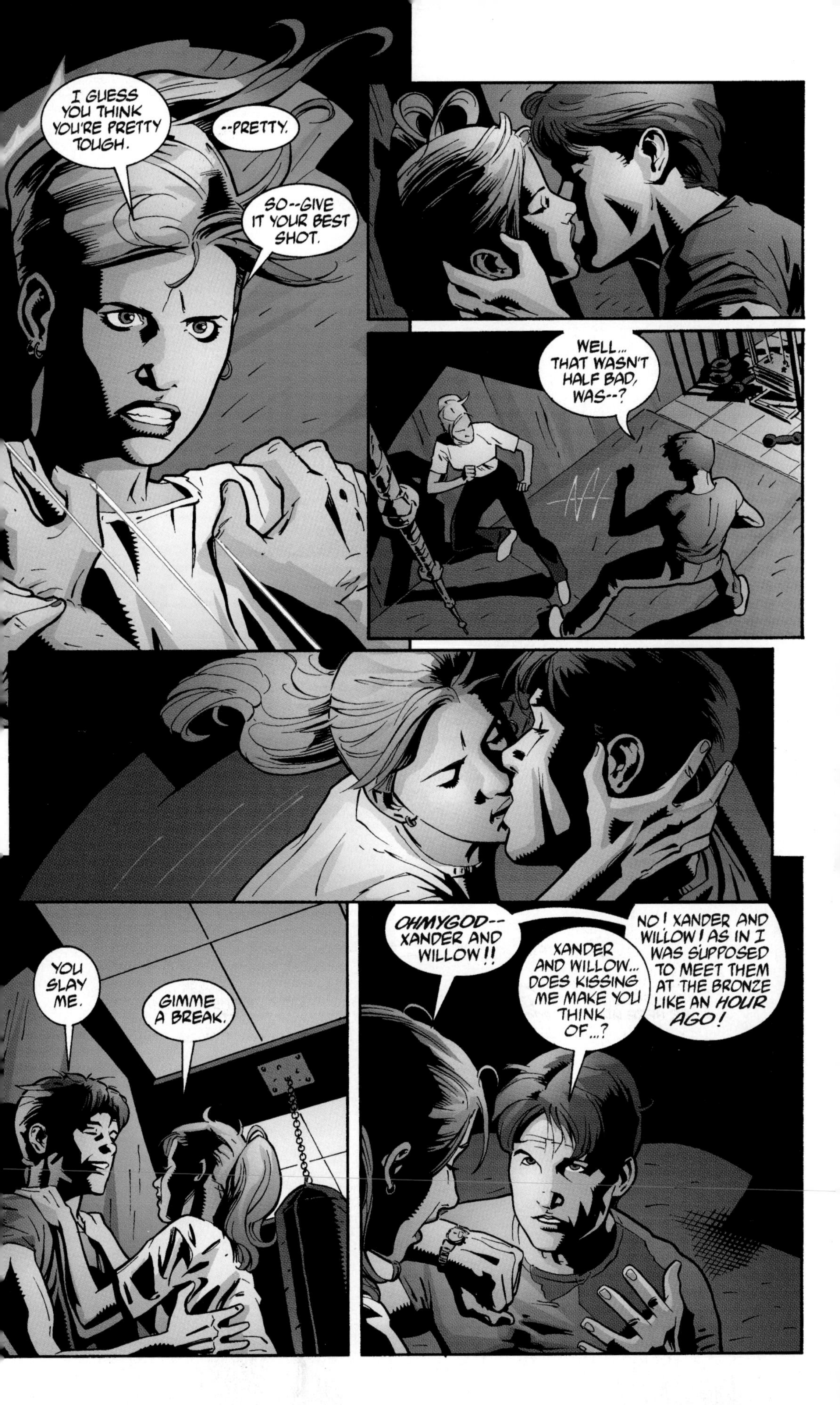

I GUESS YOU THINK YOU'RE PRETTY TOUGH.
--PRETTY.
SO--GIVE IT YOUR BEST SHOT.
WELL... THAT WASN'T HALF BAD, WAS--?
YOU SLAY ME.
GIMME A BREAK.
XANDER AND WILLOW... DOES KISSING ME MAKE YOU THINK OF...?
OHMYGOD-- XANDER AND WILLOW!!
NO! XANDER AND WILLOW! AS IN I WAS SUPPOSED TO MEET THEM AT THE BRONZE LIKE AN HOUR AGO!

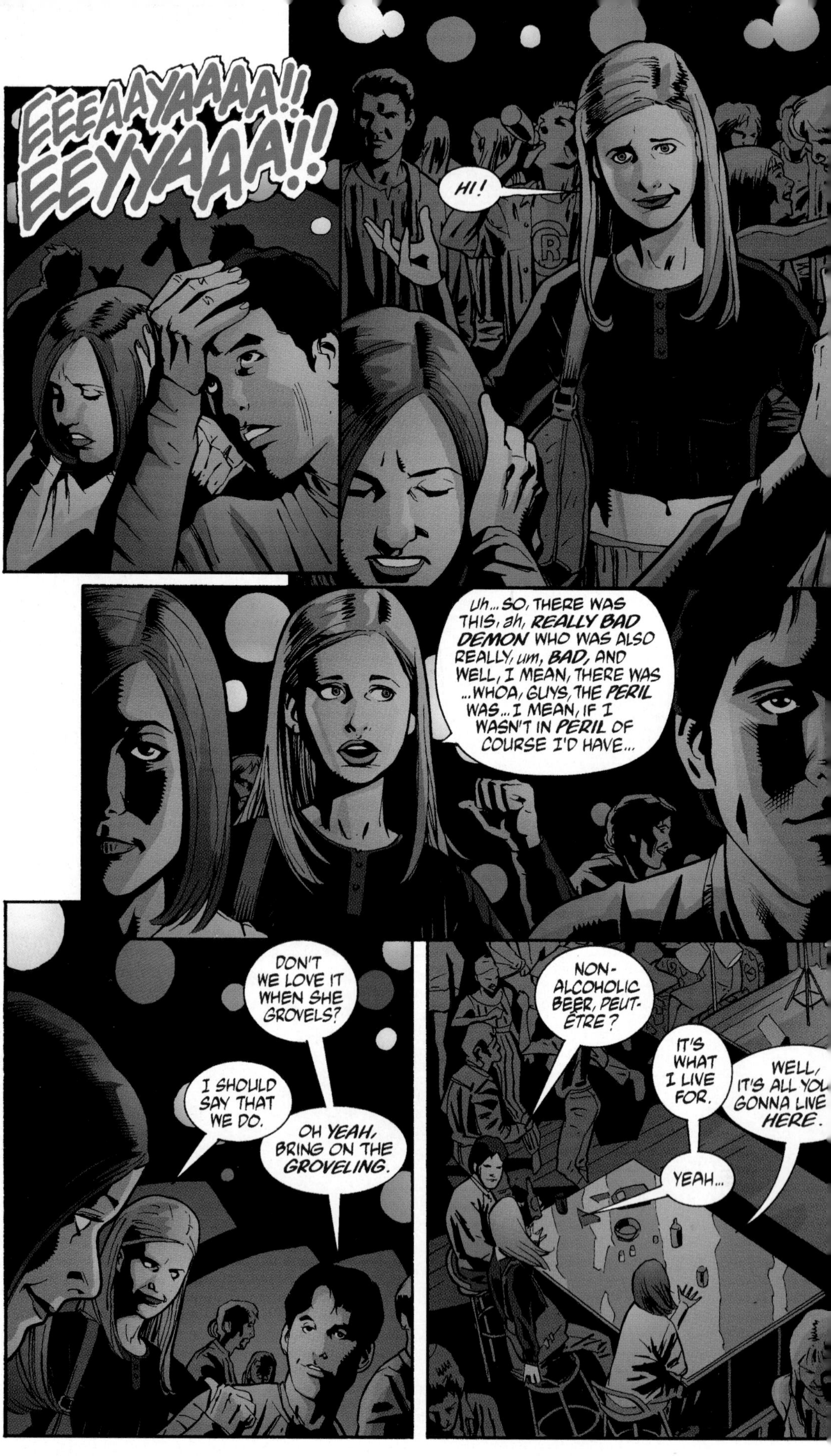
EEEAAYAAAA!! EEYYAAA!!
HI!
Uh... SO, THERE WAS THIS, ah, REALLY BAD DEMON WHO WAS ALSO REALLY, um, BAD, AND WELL, I MEAN, THERE WAS ...WHOA, GUYS, THE PERIL WAS... I MEAN, IF I WASN'T IN PERIL OF COURSE I'D HAVE...
DON'T WE LOVE IT WHEN SHE GROVELS?
I SHOULD SAY THAT WE DO.
OH YEAH, BRING ON THE GROVELING.
NON-ALCOHOLIC BEER, PEUT-ÊTRE?
IT'S WHAT I LIVE FOR.
WELL, IT'S ALL YOU GONNA LIVE HERE.
YEAH...

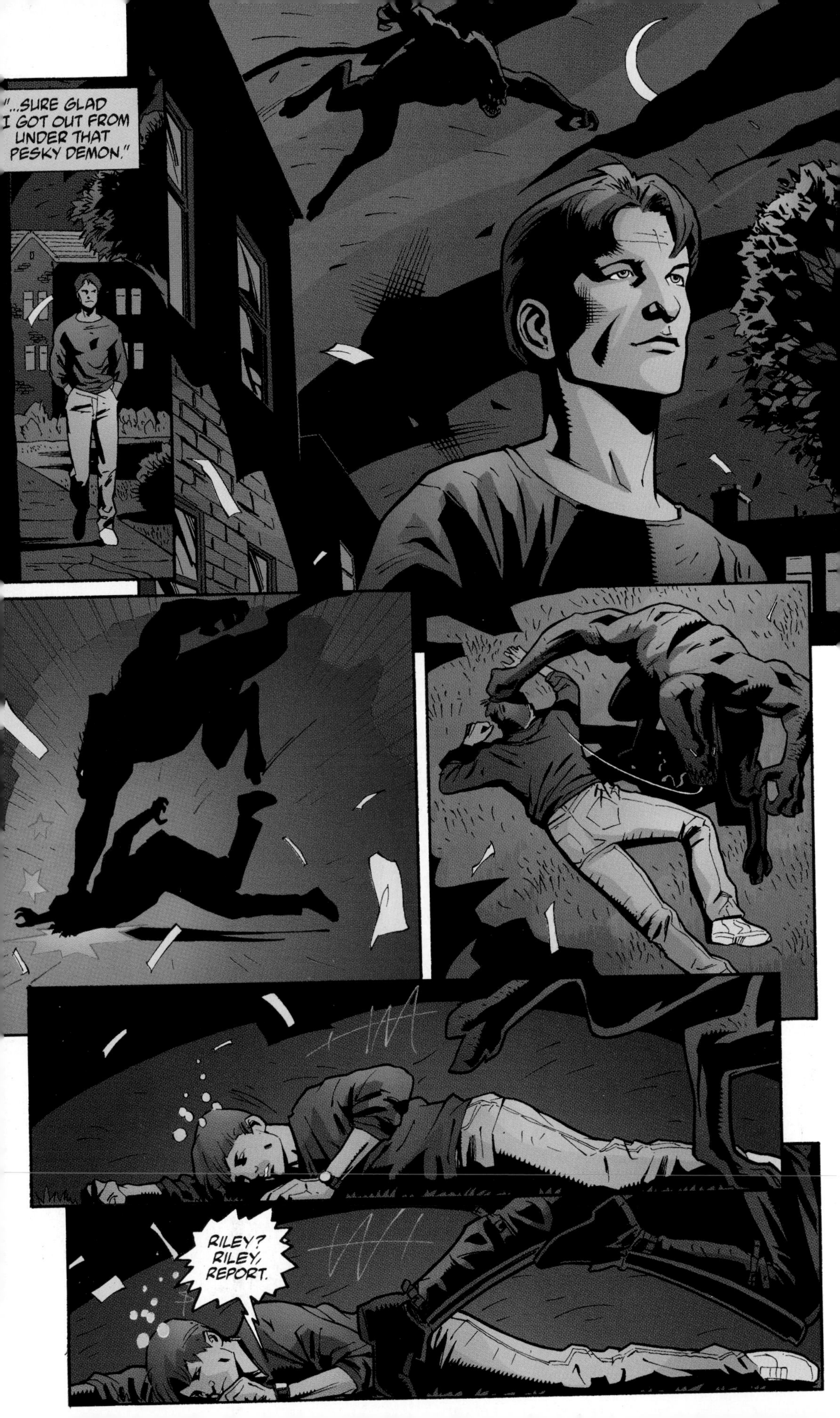
"...SURE GLAD I GOT OUT FROM UNDER THAT PESKY DEMON."
RILEY? RILEY, REPORT.

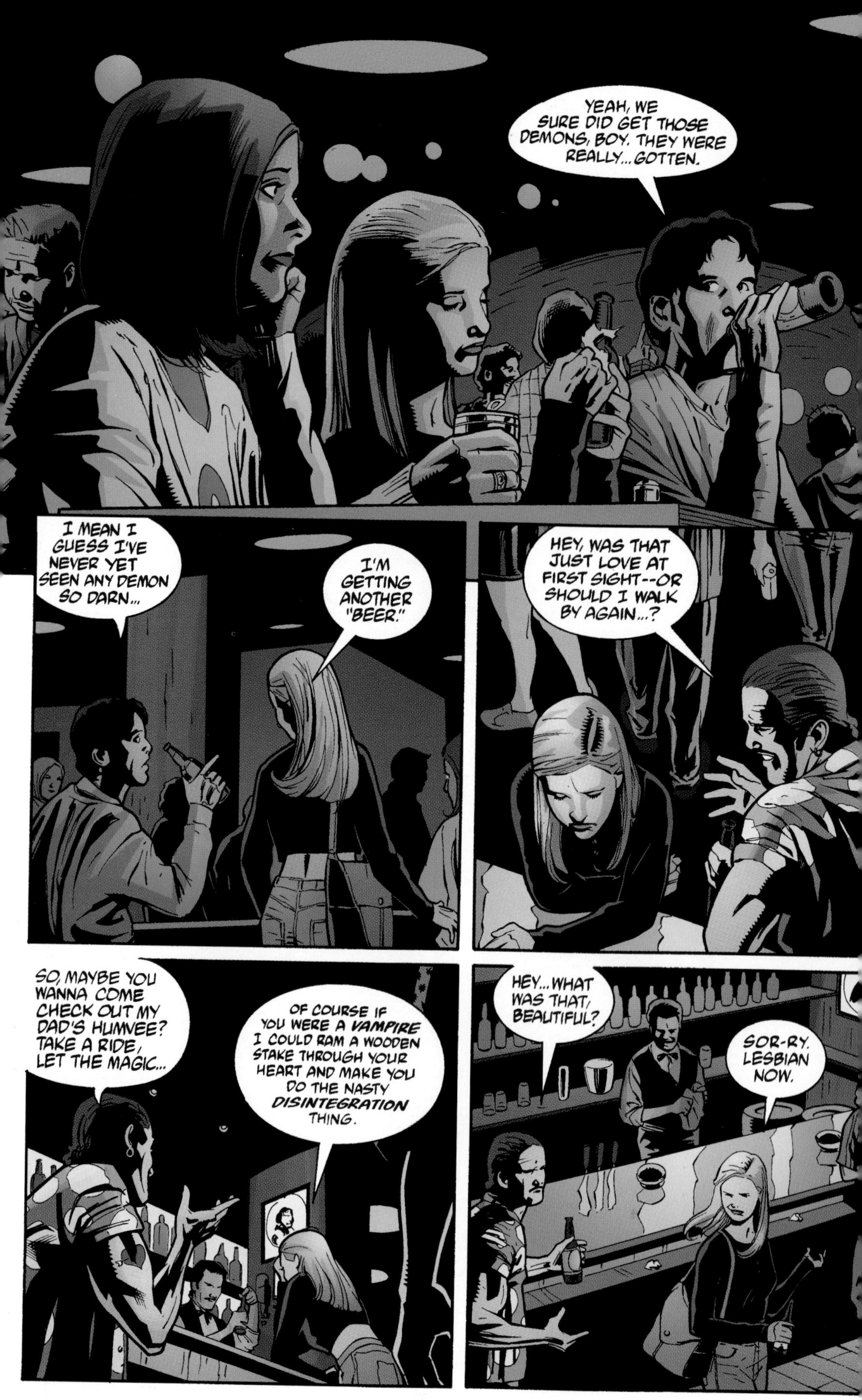
YEAH, WE SURE DID GET THOSE DEMONS, BOY. THEY WERE REALLY... GOTTEN.
I MEAN I GUESS I'VE NEVER YET SEEN ANY DEMON SO DARN...
I'M GETTING ANOTHER "BEER."
HEY, WAS THAT JUST LOVE AT FIRST SIGHT--OR SHOULD I WALK BY AGAIN...?
SO, MAYBE YOU WANNA COME CHECK OUT MY DAD'S HUMVEE? TAKE A RIDE, LET THE MAGIC...
OF COURSE IF YOU WERE A *VAMPIRE* I COULD RAM A WOODEN STAKE THROUGH YOUR HEART AND MAKE YOU DO THE NASTY *DISINTEGRATION* THING.
HEY... WHAT WAS THAT, BEAUTIFUL?
SOR-RY. LESBIAN NOW.

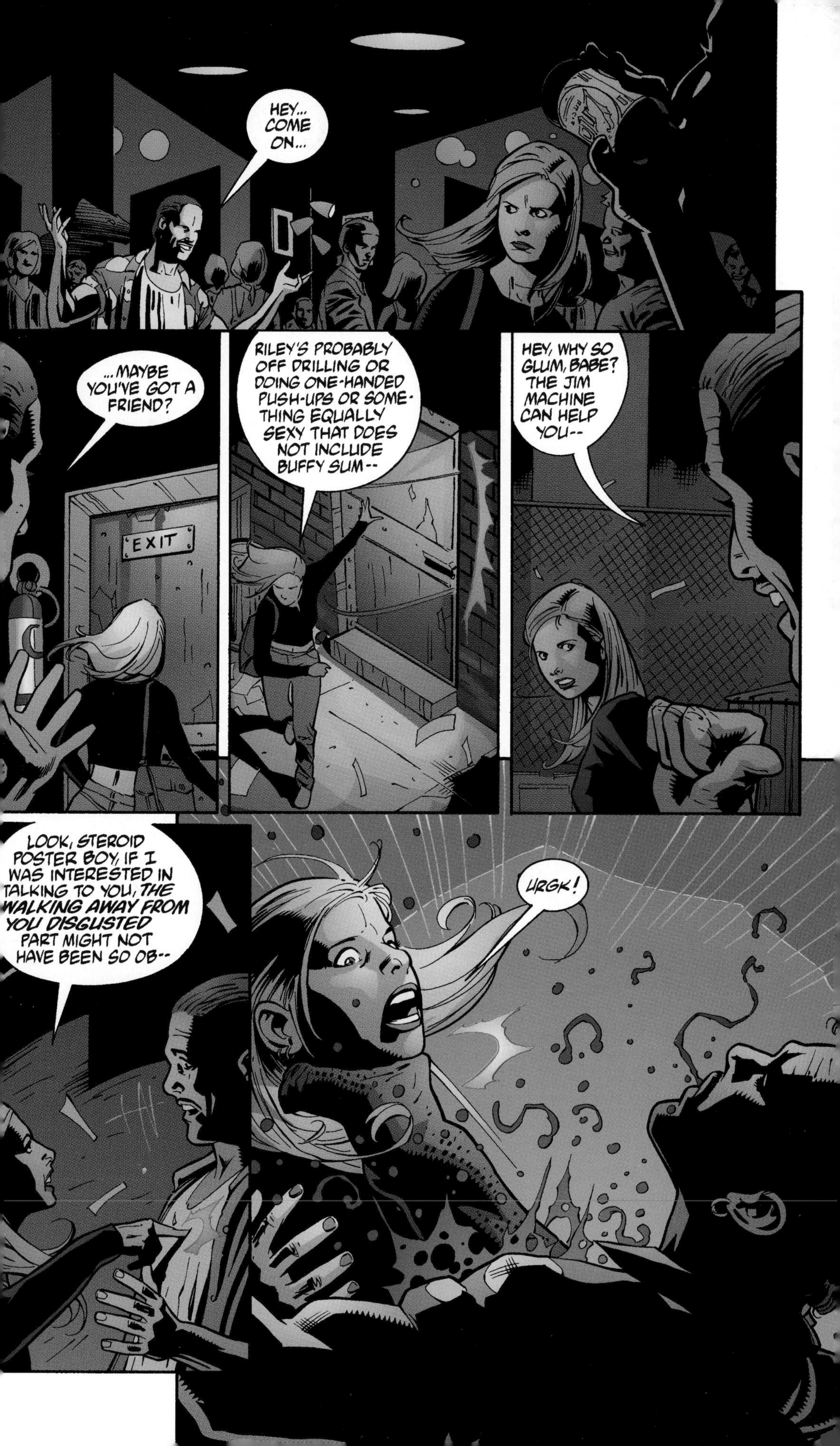
HEY... COME ON...
...MAYBE YOU'VE GOT A FRIEND?
RILEY'S PROBABLY OFF DRILLING OR DOING ONE-HANDED PUSH-UPS OR SOMETHING EQUALLY SEXY THAT DOES NOT INCLUDE BUFFY SUM--
HEY, WHY SO GLUM, BABE? THE JIM MACHINE CAN HELP YOU--
LOOK, STEROID POSTER BOY, IF I WAS INTERESTED IN TALKING TO YOU, THE WALKING AWAY FROM YOU DISGUSTED PART MIGHT NOT HAVE BEEN SO OB--
URGK!

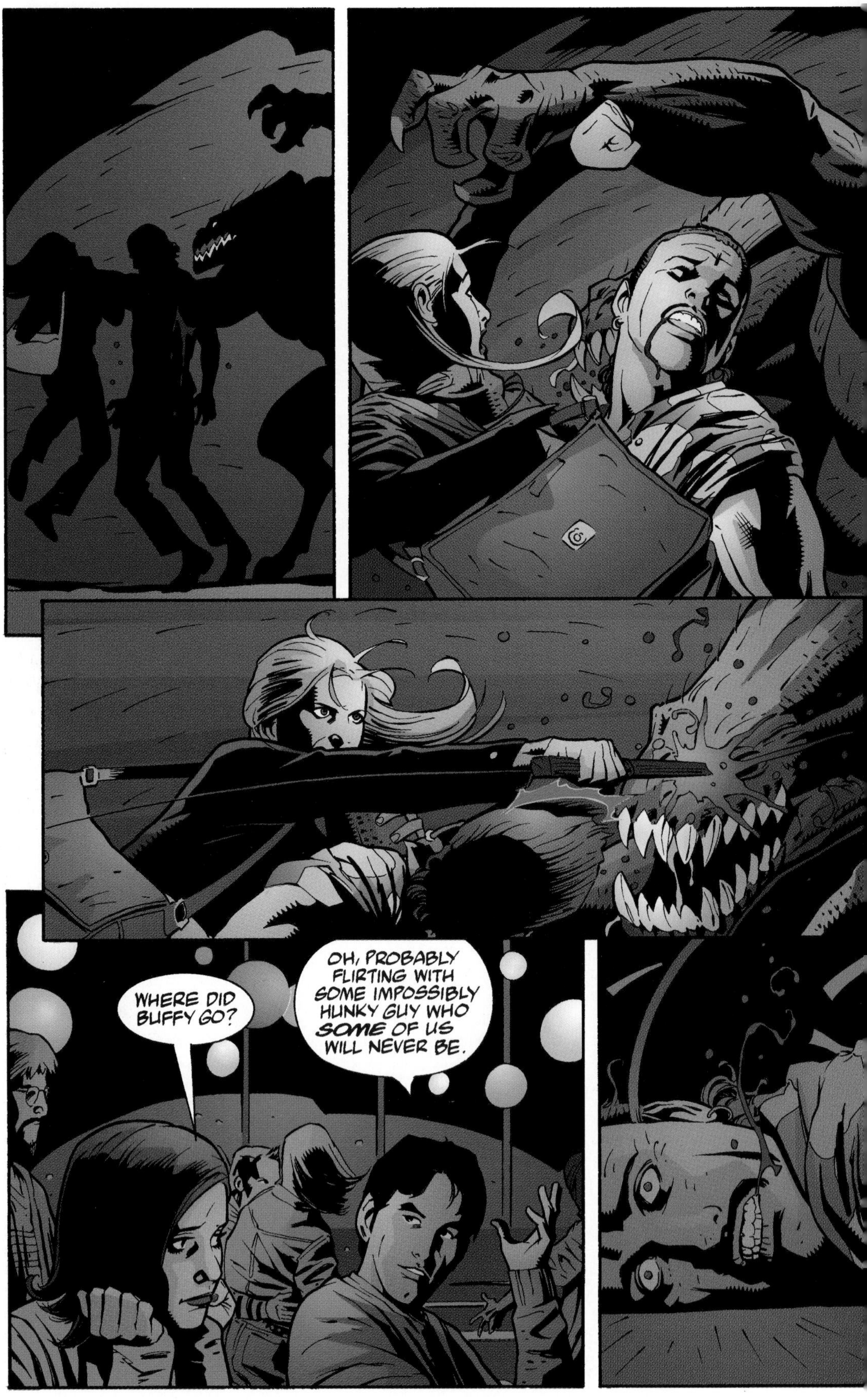
WHERE DID BUFFY GO?
OH, PROBABLY FLIRTING WITH SOME IMPOSSIBLY HUNKY GUY WHO SOME OF US WILL NEVER BE.

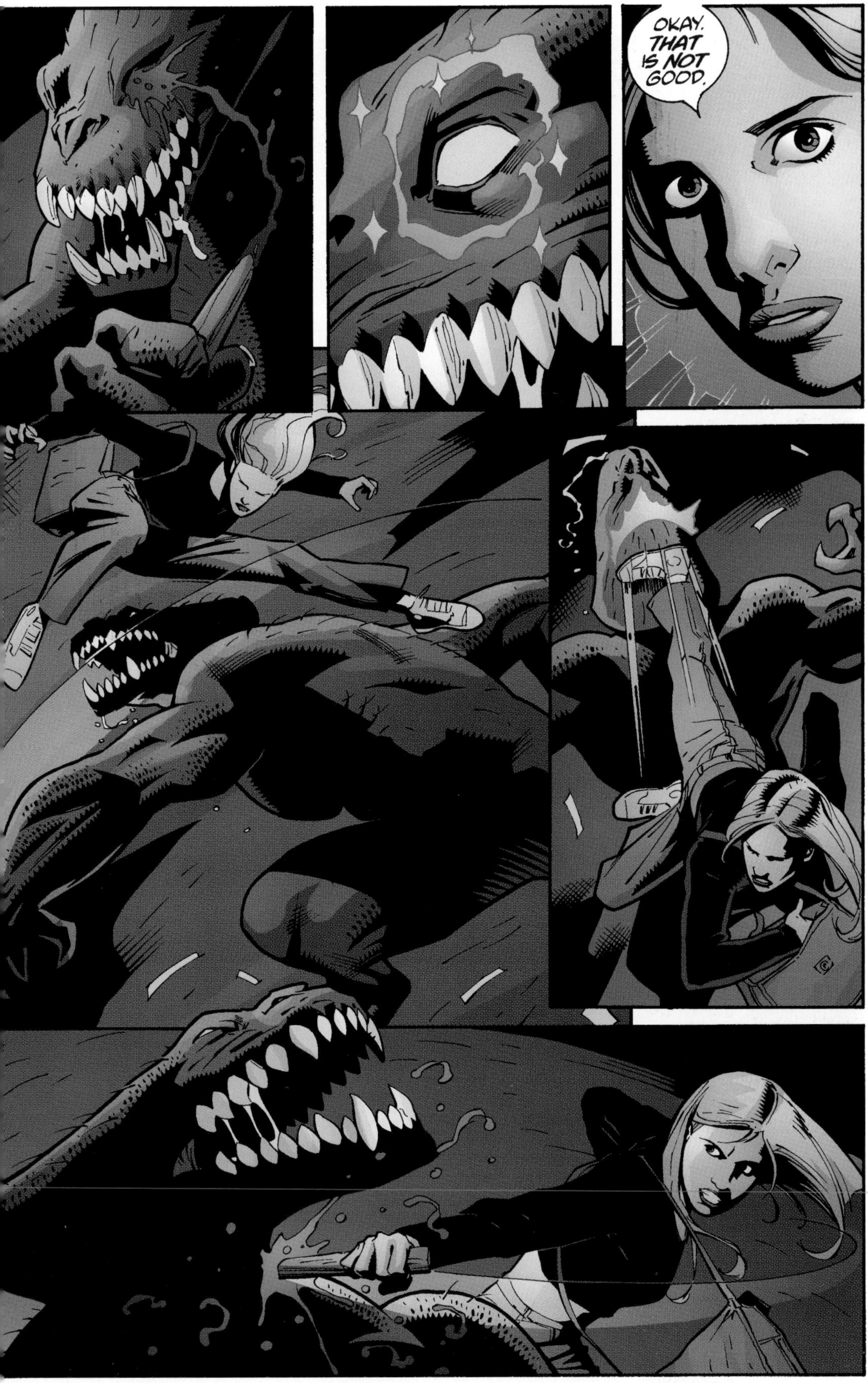
OKAY. THAT IS NOT GOOD.

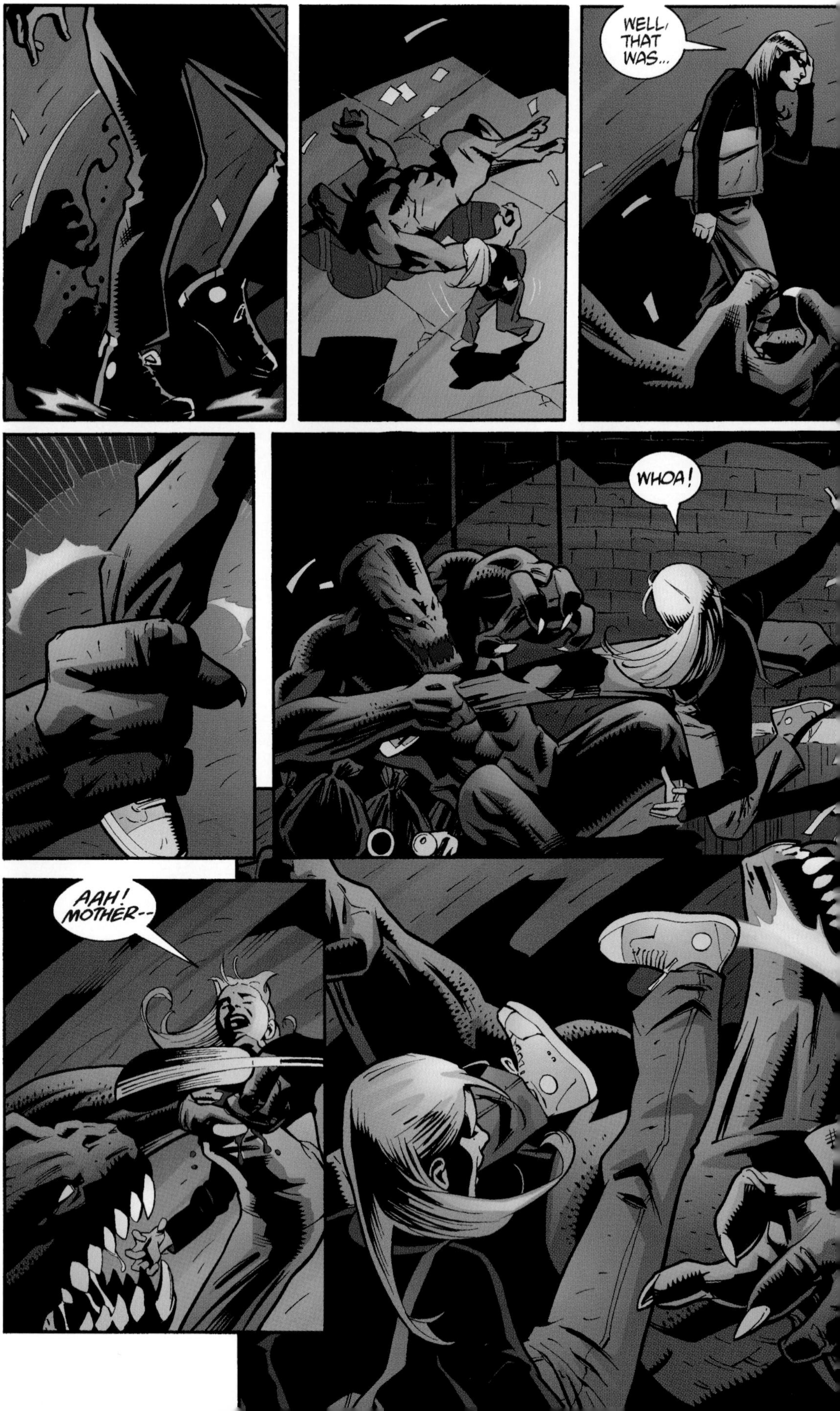
WELL, THAT WAS...
WHOA!
AAH! MOTHER--

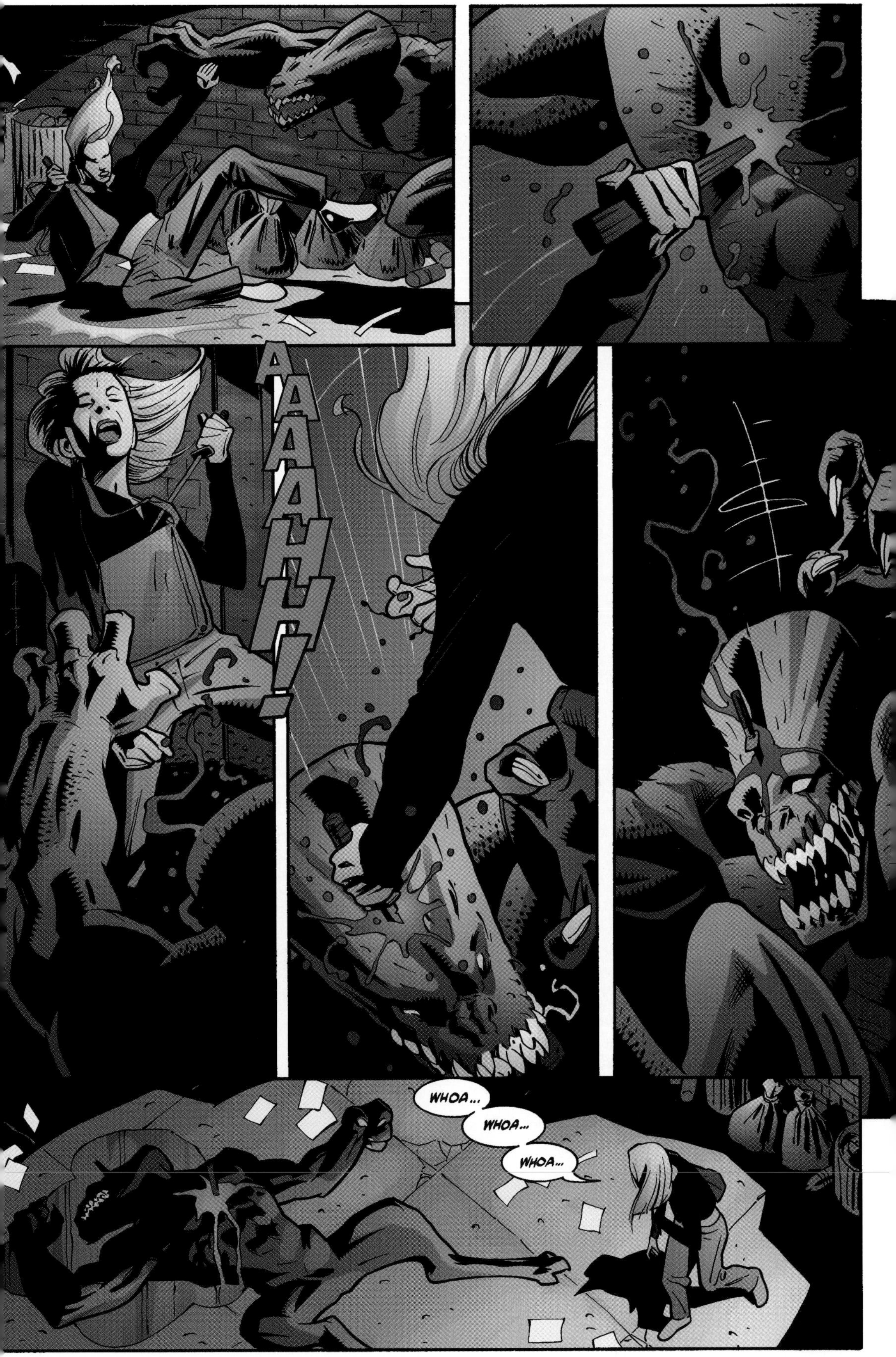

AAAAHH!!
WHOA...
WHOA...
WHOA...

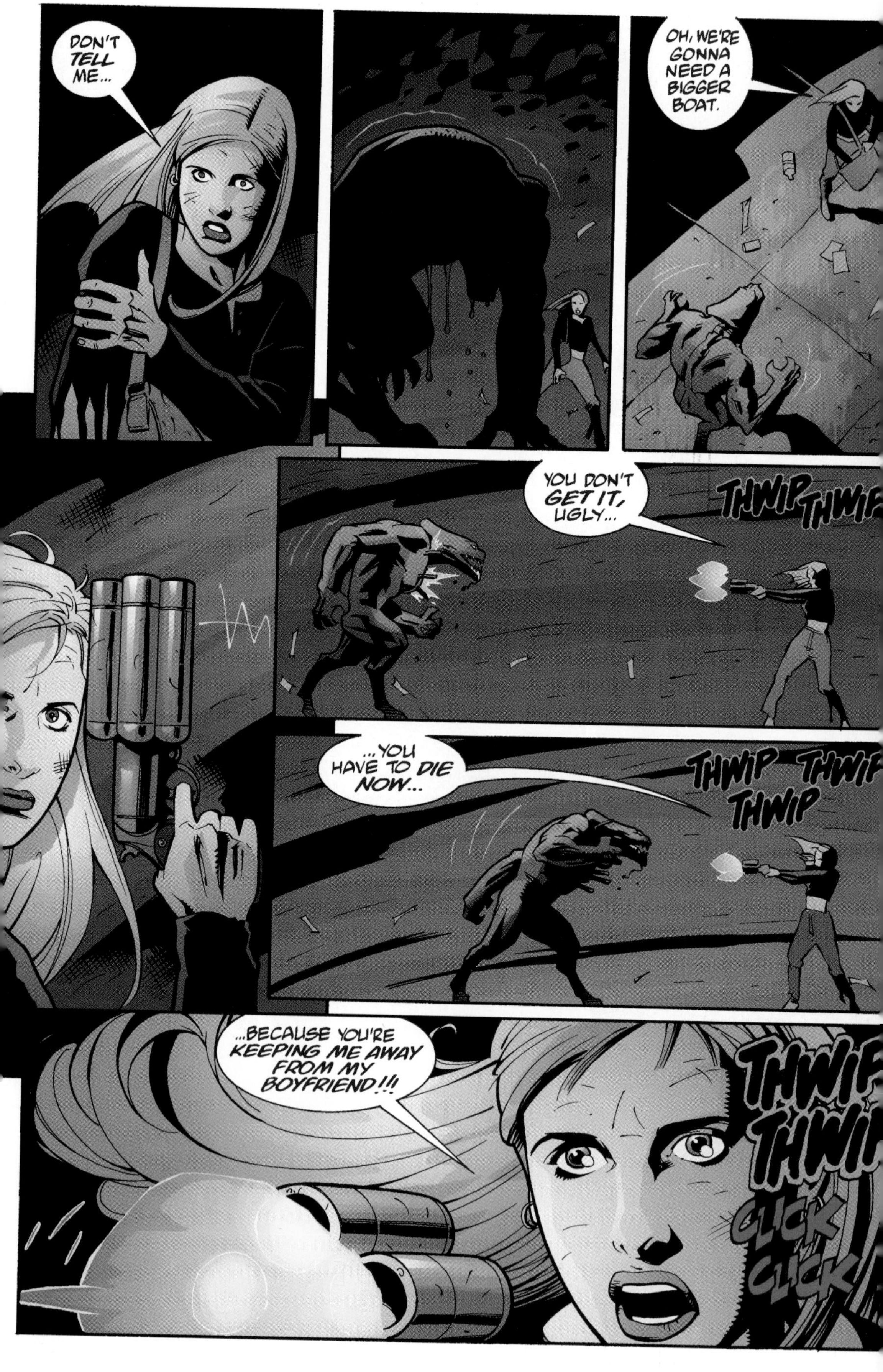
DON'T TELL ME...
OH, WE'RE GONNA NEED A BIGGER BOAT.
YOU DON'T GET IT, UGLY...
THWIP THWIP
...YOU HAVE TO DIE NOW...
THWIP THWIP THWIP
...BECAUSE YOU'RE KEEPING ME AWAY FROM MY BOYFRIEND!!!
THWIP THWIP
CLICK CLICK

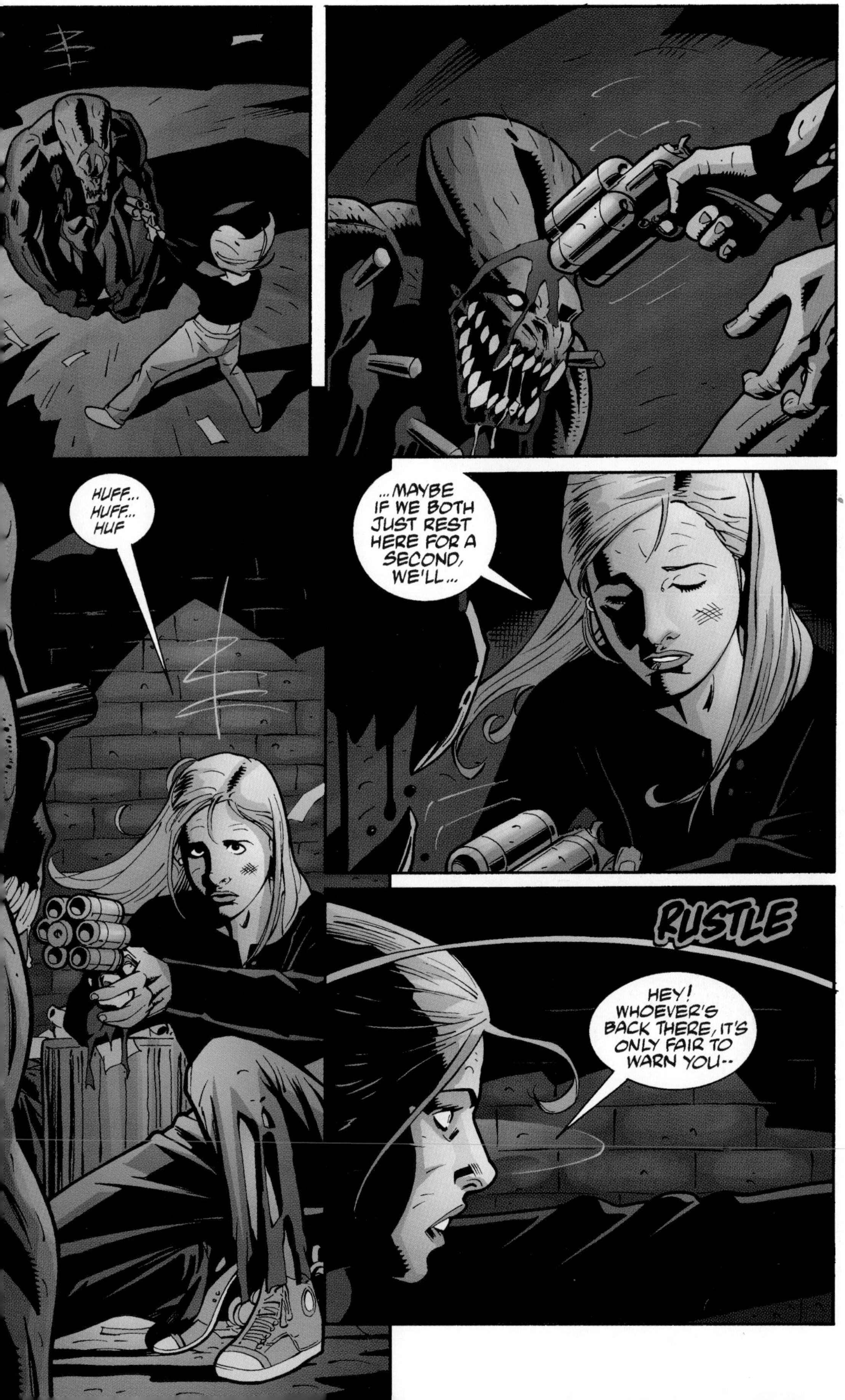
HUFF... HUFF... HUF
...MAYBE IF WE BOTH JUST REST HERE FOR A SECOND, WE'LL...
RUSTLE
HEY! WHOEVER'S BACK THERE, IT'S ONLY FAIR TO WARN YOU--

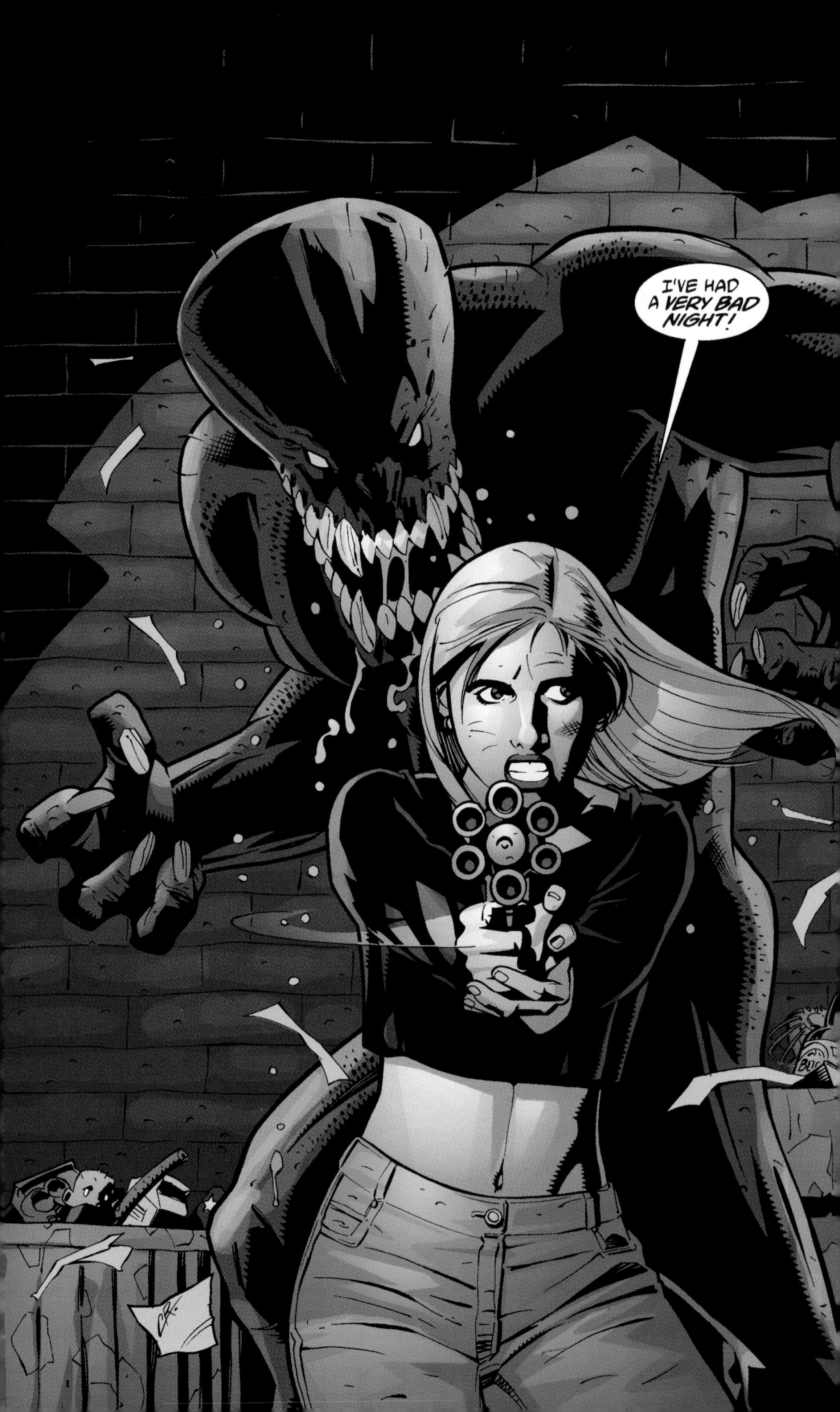
I'VE HAD A VERY BAD NIGHT!

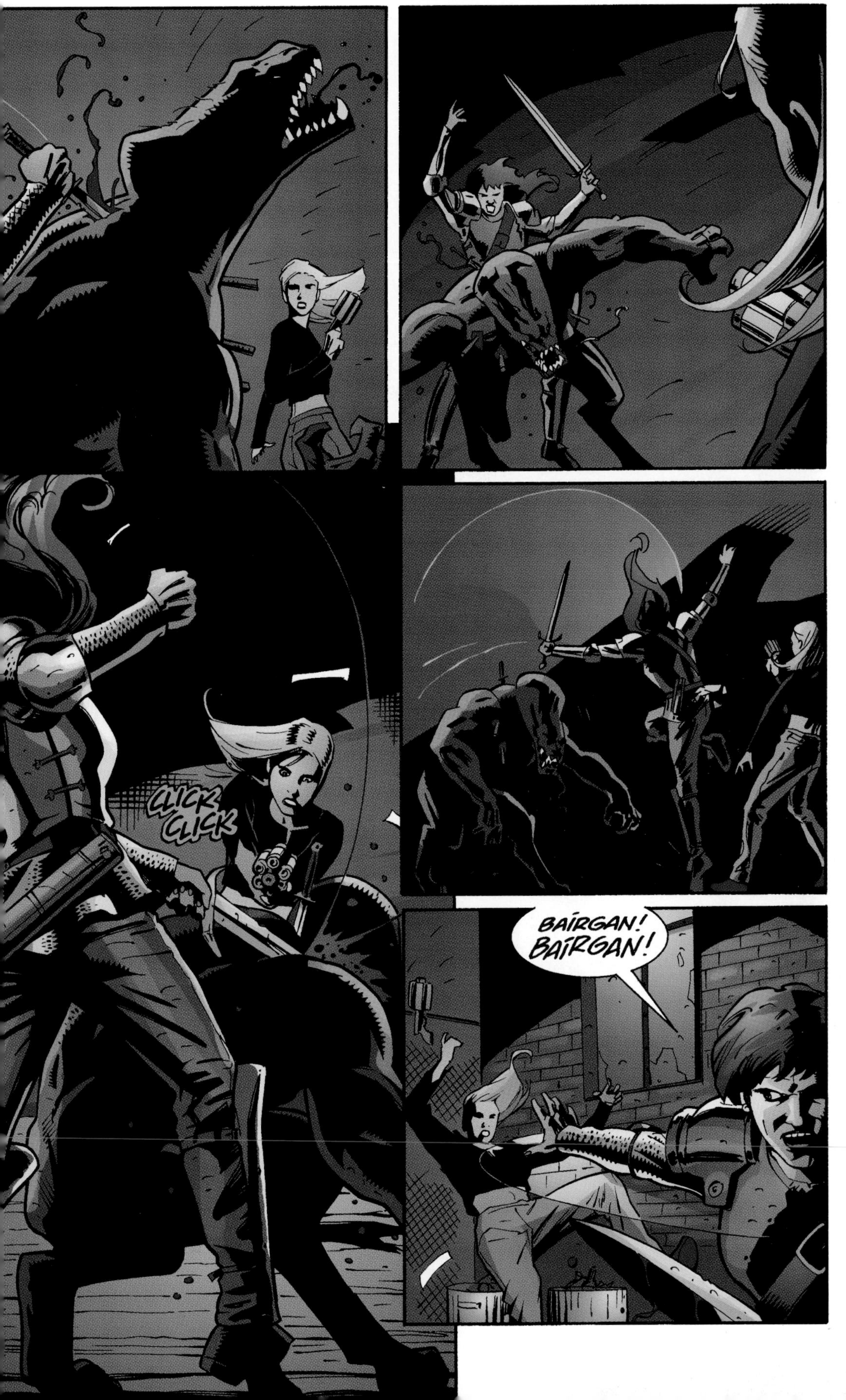
CLICK CLICK
BAIRGAN! BAIRGAN!

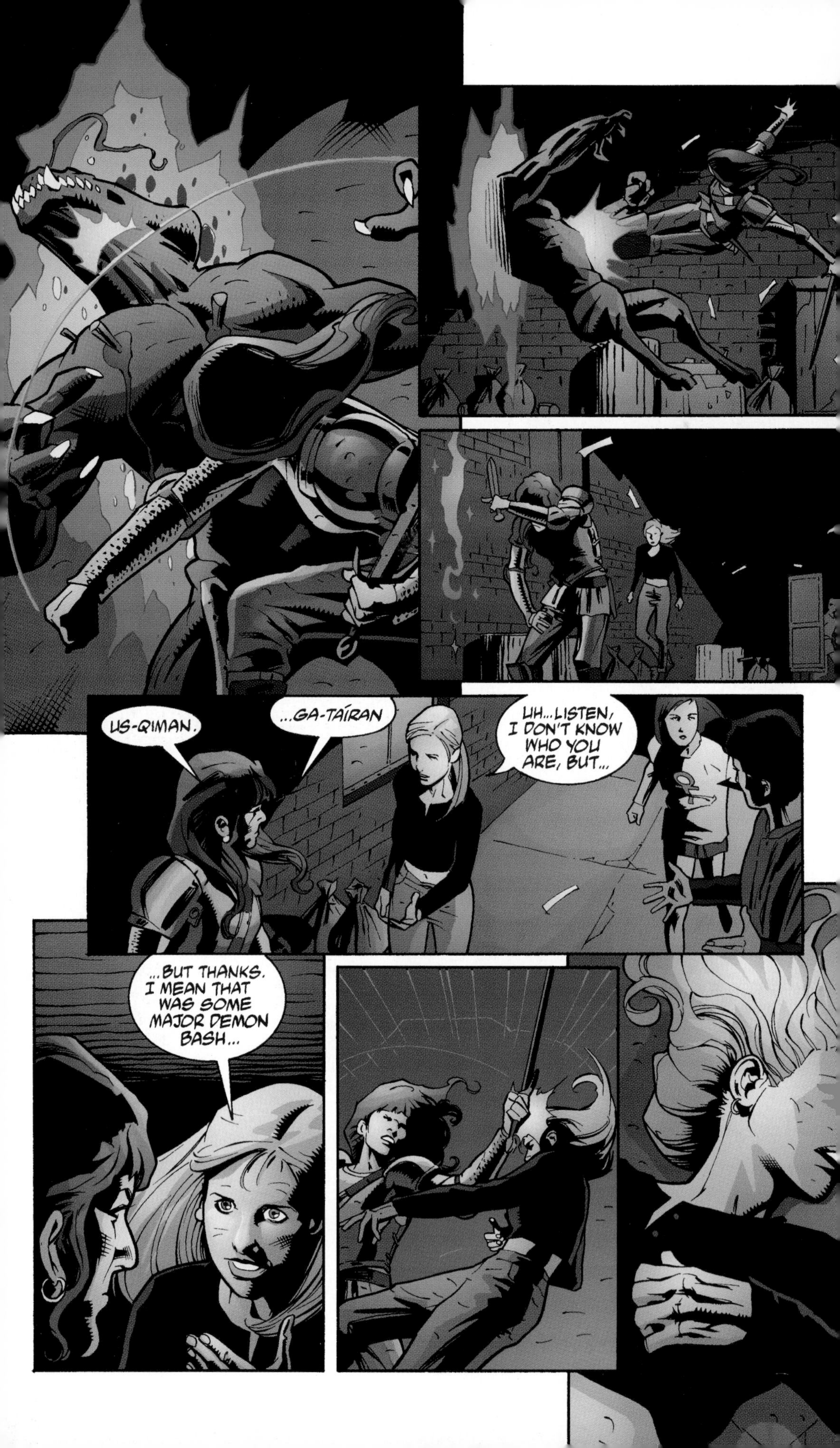
US-QIMAN.
...GA-TAÍRAN
UH...LISTEN, I DON'T KNOW WHO YOU ARE, BUT...
...BUT THANKS. I MEAN THAT WAS SOME MAJOR DEMON BASH...

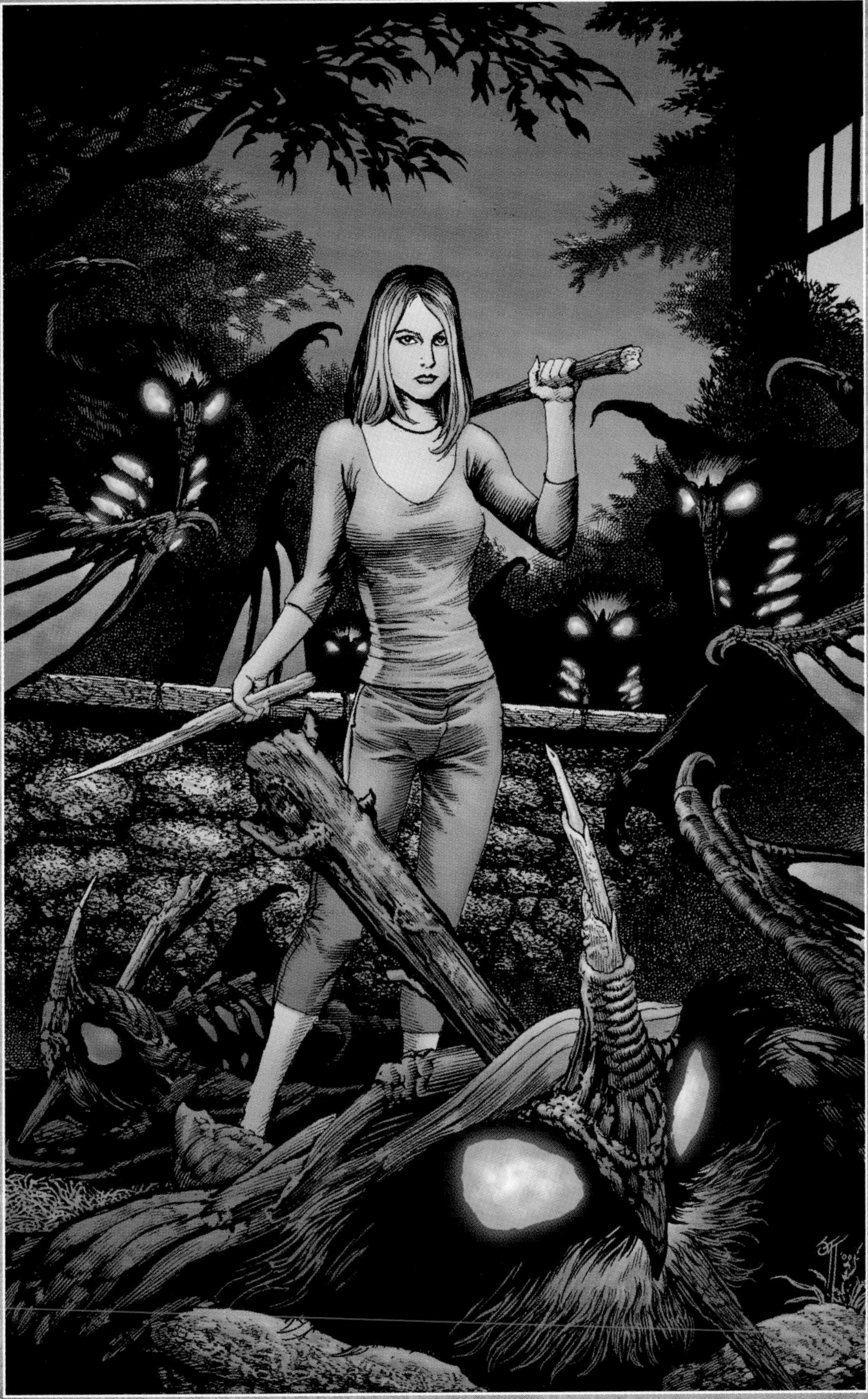

Art by JOHN TOTLEBEN
with DAVE STEWART

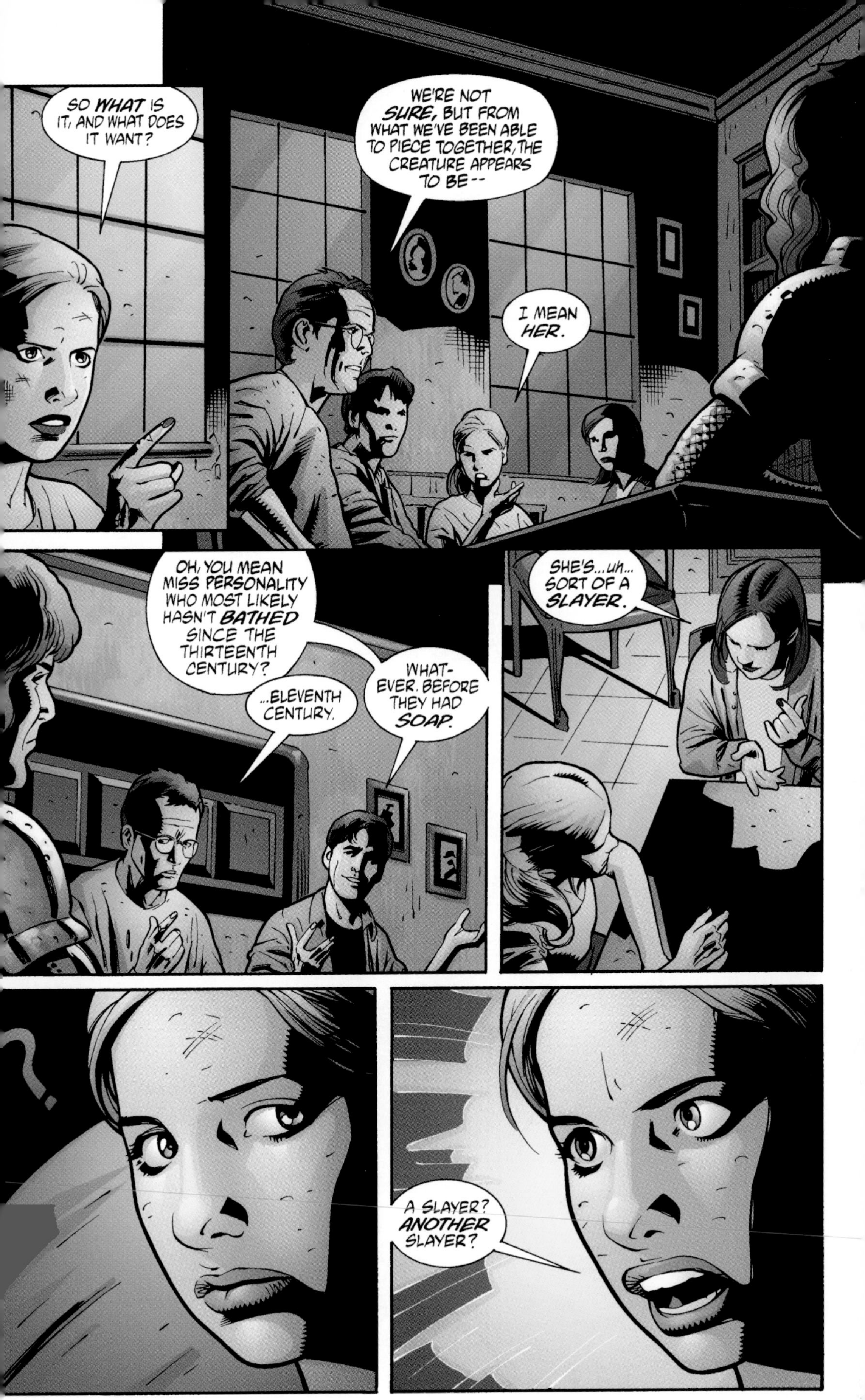
SO WHAT IS IT, AND WHAT DOES IT WANT?
WE'RE NOT SURE, BUT FROM WHAT WE'VE BEEN ABLE TO PIECE TOGETHER, THE CREATURE APPEARS TO BE--
I MEAN HER.
OH, YOU MEAN MISS PERSONALITY WHO MOST LIKELY HASN'T BATHED SINCE THE THIRTEENTH CENTURY?
...ELEVENTH CENTURY.
WHAT-EVER. BEFORE THEY HAD SOAP.
SHE'S...uh... SORT OF A SLAYER.
A SLAYER? ANOTHER SLAYER?

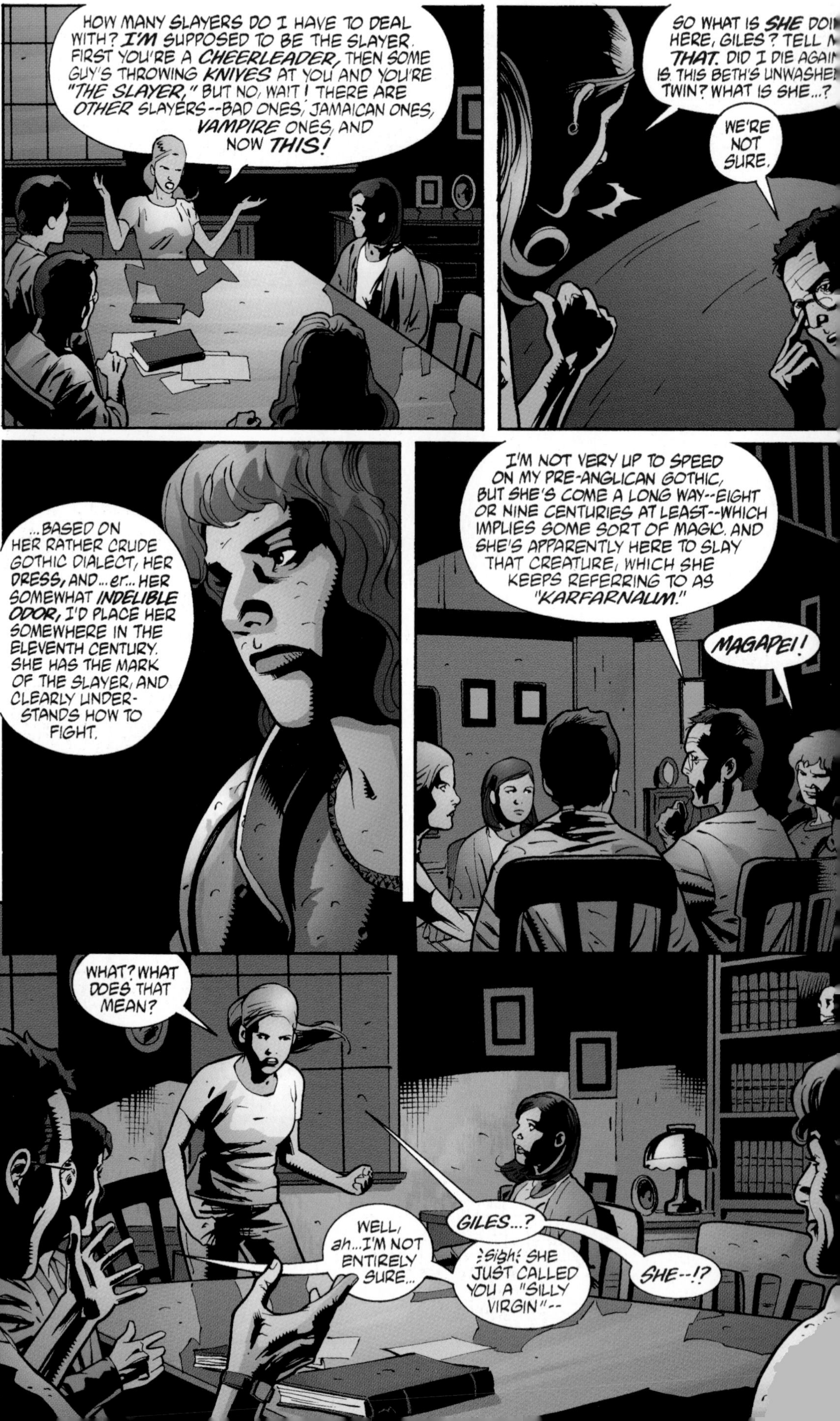
HOW MANY SLAYERS DO I HAVE TO DEAL WITH? I'M SUPPOSED TO BE THE SLAYER. FIRST YOU'RE A CHEERLEADER, THEN SOME GUY'S THROWING KNIVES AT YOU AND YOU'RE "THE SLAYER," BUT NO, WAIT! THERE ARE OTHER SLAYERS--BAD ONES, JAMAICAN ONES, VAMPIRE ONES, AND NOW THIS!
SO WHAT IS SHE DOI HERE, GILES? TELL M THAT. DID I DIE AGAI IS THIS BETH'S UNWASHE TWIN? WHAT IS SHE...?
WE'RE NOT SURE.
...BASED ON HER RATHER CRUDE GOTHIC DIALECT, HER DRESS, AND... er... HER SOMEWHAT INDELIBLE ODOR, I'D PLACE HER SOMEWHERE IN THE ELEVENTH CENTURY. SHE HAS THE MARK OF THE SLAYER, AND CLEARLY UNDER-STANDS HOW TO FIGHT.
I'M NOT VERY UP TO SPEED ON MY PRE-ANGLICAN GOTHIC, BUT SHE'S COME A LONG WAY--EIGHT OR NINE CENTURIES AT LEAST--WHICH IMPLIES SOME SORT OF MAGIC. AND SHE'S APPARENTLY HERE TO SLAY THAT CREATURE, WHICH SHE KEEPS REFERRING TO AS "KARFARNAUM."
MAGAPEI!
WHAT? WHAT DOES THAT MEAN?
WELL, ah... I'M NOT ENTIRELY SURE...
GILES...?
:sigh: SHE JUST CALLED YOU A "SILLY VIRGIN"--
SHE--!?

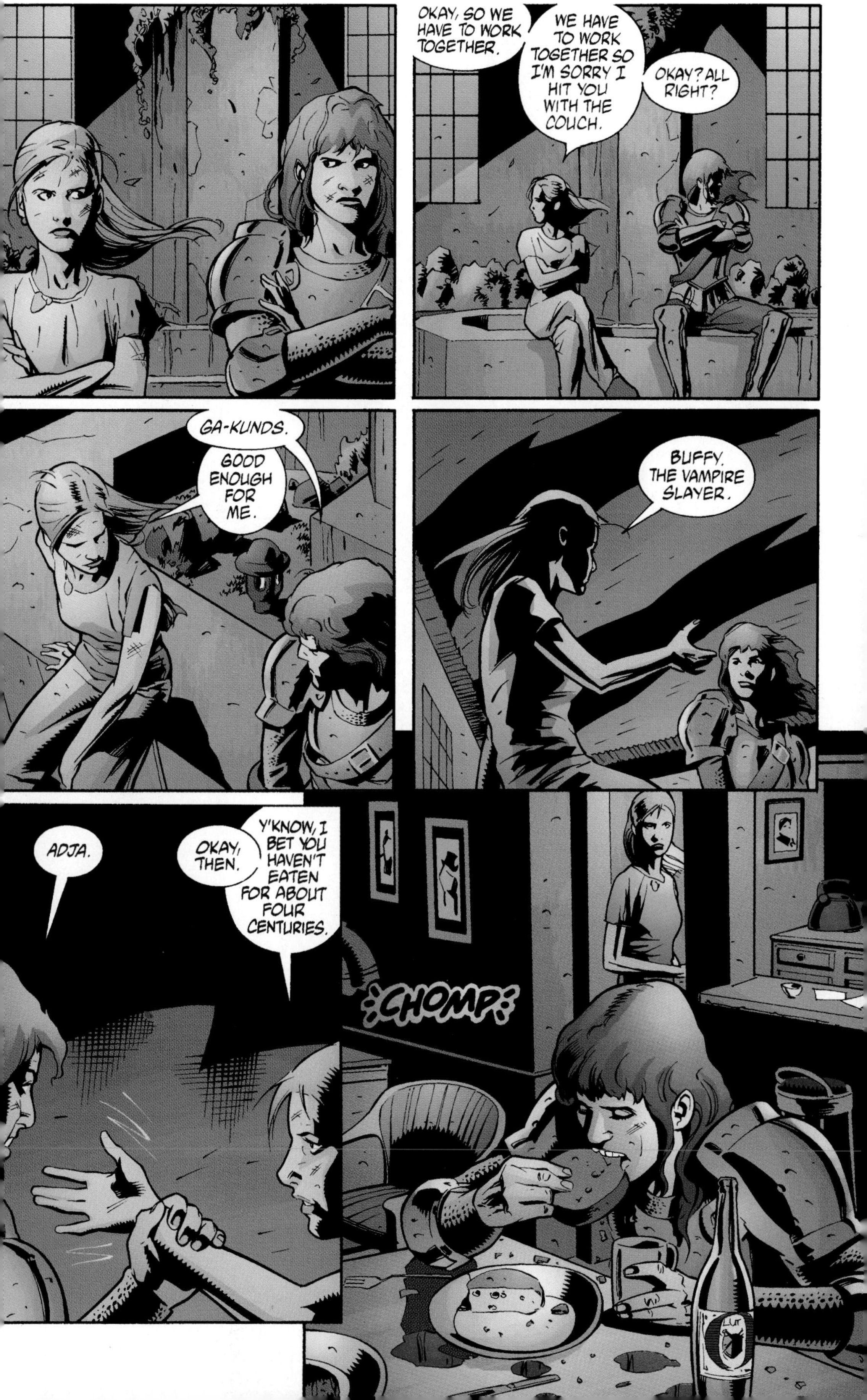
OKAY, SO WE HAVE TO WORK TOGETHER.
WE HAVE TO WORK TOGETHER SO I'M SORRY I HIT YOU WITH THE COUCH.
OKAY? ALL RIGHT?
GA-KUNDS.
GOOD ENOUGH FOR ME.
BUFFY. THE VAMPIRE SLAYER.
ADJA.
OKAY, THEN.
Y'KNOW, I BET YOU HAVEN'T EATEN FOR ABOUT FOUR CENTURIES.
CHOMP

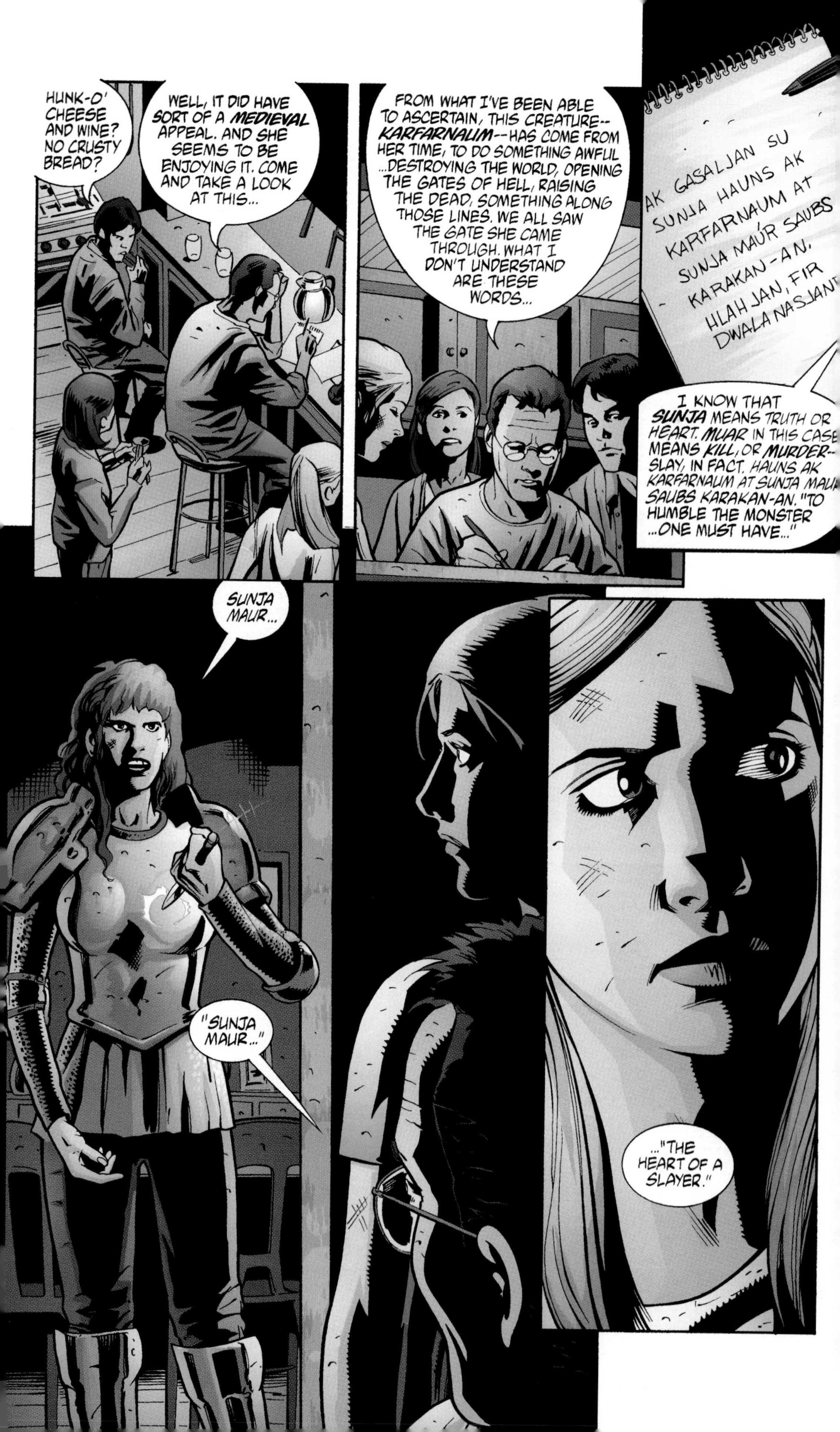
HUNK-O' CHEESE AND WINE? NO CRUSTY BREAD?
WELL, IT DID HAVE SORT OF A MEDIEVAL APPEAL. AND SHE SEEMS TO BE ENJOYING IT. COME AND TAKE A LOOK AT THIS...
FROM WHAT I'VE BEEN ABLE TO ASCERTAIN, THIS CREATURE-- KARFARNAUM--HAS COME FROM HER TIME, TO DO SOMETHING AWFUL ...DESTROYING THE WORLD, OPENING THE GATES OF HELL, RAISING THE DEAD, SOMETHING ALONG THOSE LINES. WE ALL SAW THE GATE SHE CAME THROUGH. WHAT I DON'T UNDERSTAND ARE THESE WORDS...
AK GASALJAN SU SUNJA HAUNS AK KARFARNAUM AT SUNJA MAÚR SAUBS SUNJA KARAKAN-AN, HLAH JAN, FIR DWALA NASJANT
I KNOW THAT SUNJA MEANS TRUTH OR HEART. MUAR IN THIS CASE MEANS KILL, OR MURDER-- SLAY, IN FACT. HAUNS AK KARFARNAUM AT SUNJA MAUR SAUBS KARAKAN-AN. "TO HUMBLE THE MONSTER ...ONE MUST HAVE..."
SUNJA MAUR...
"SUNJA MAUR..."
..."THE HEART OF A SLAYER."

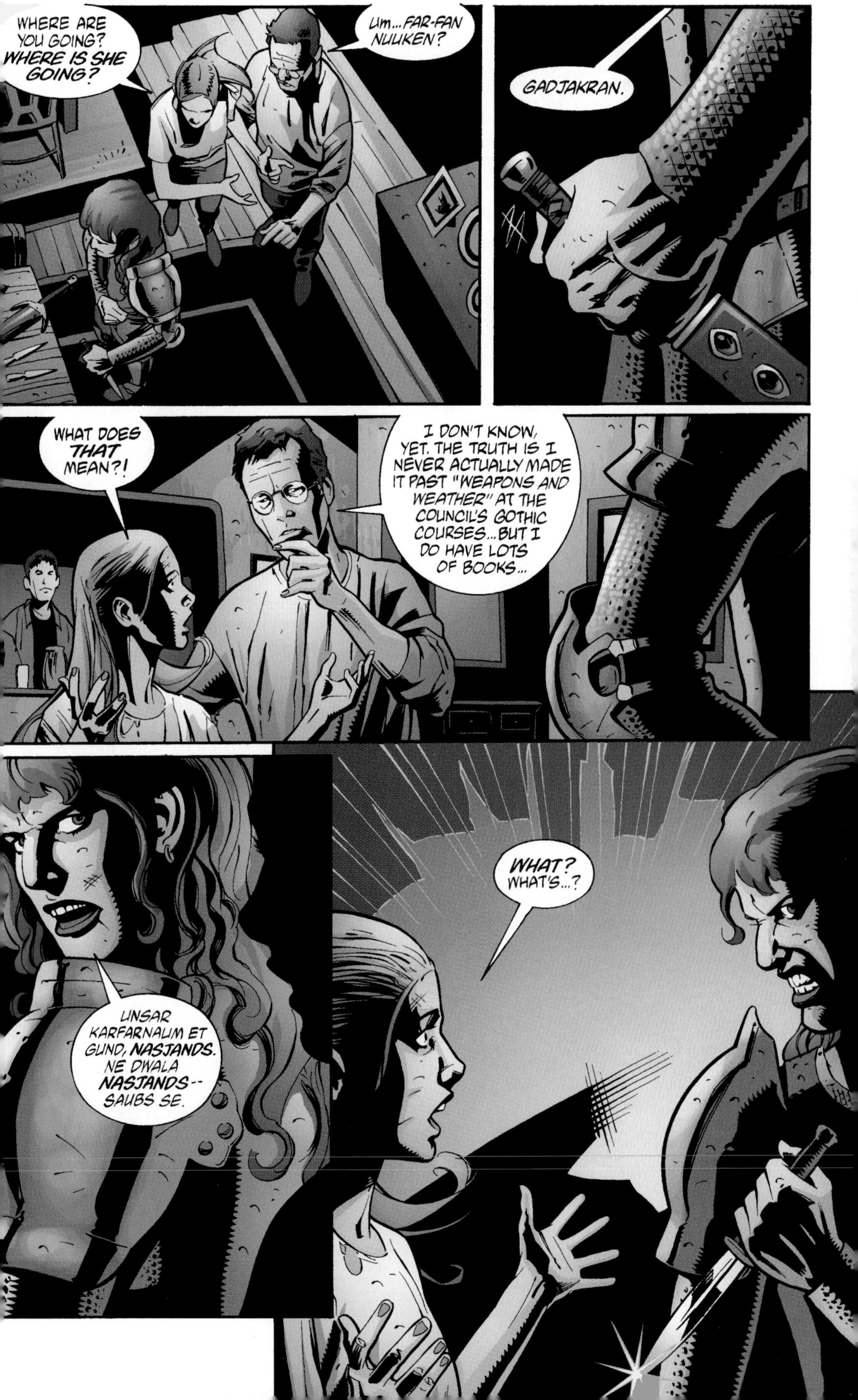
WHERE ARE YOU GOING? WHERE IS SHE GOING?
UM... FAR-FAN NUUKEN?
GADJAKRAN.
WHAT DOES THAT MEAN?!
I DON'T KNOW, YET. THE TRUTH IS I NEVER ACTUALLY MADE IT PAST "WEAPONS AND WEATHER" AT THE COUNCIL'S GOTHIC COURSES... BUT I DO HAVE LOTS OF BOOKS...
UNSAR KARFARNAUM ET GUND, NASJANDS. NE DWALA NASJANDS-- SAUBS SE.
WHAT? WHAT'S...?

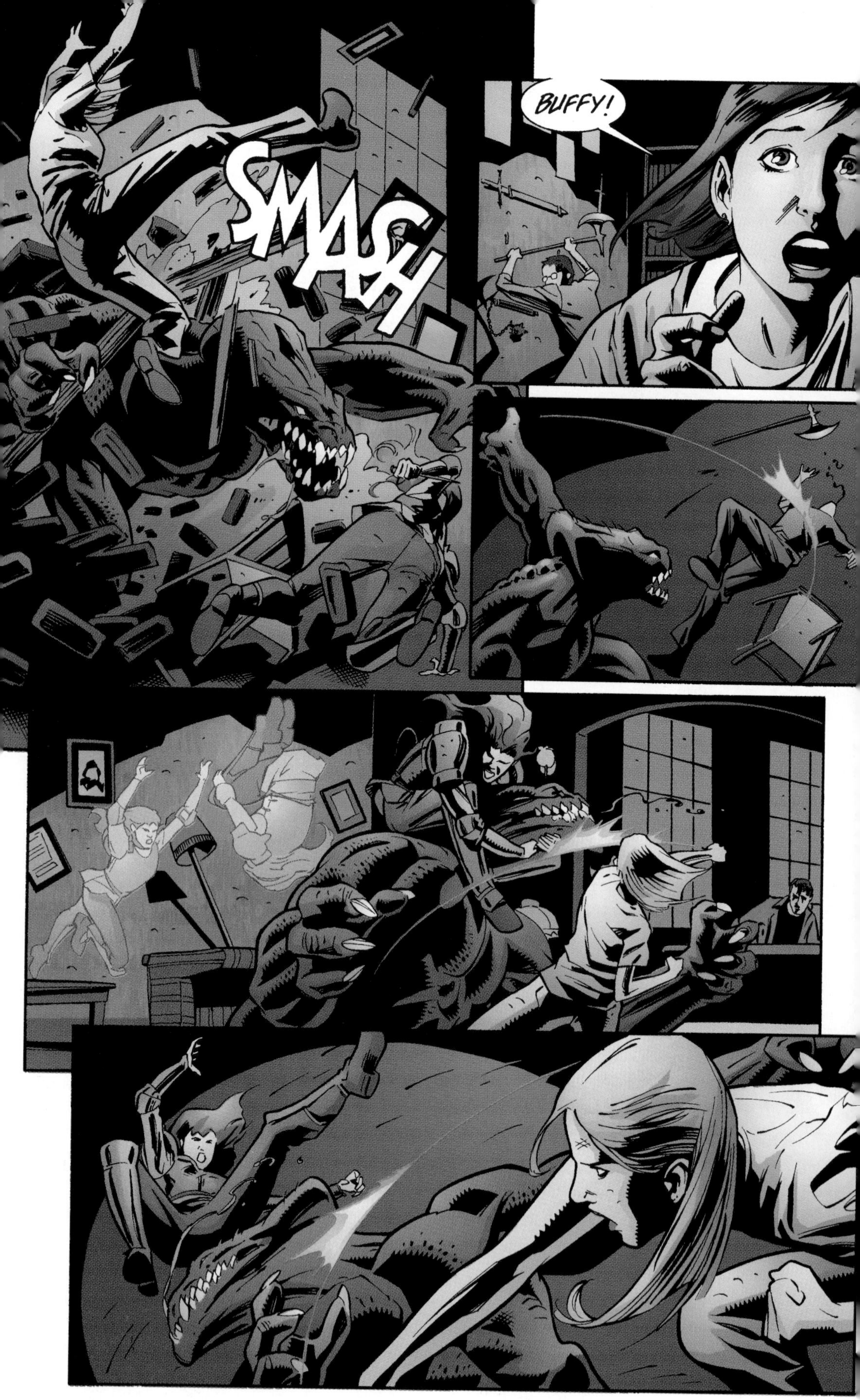
SMASH
BUFFY!

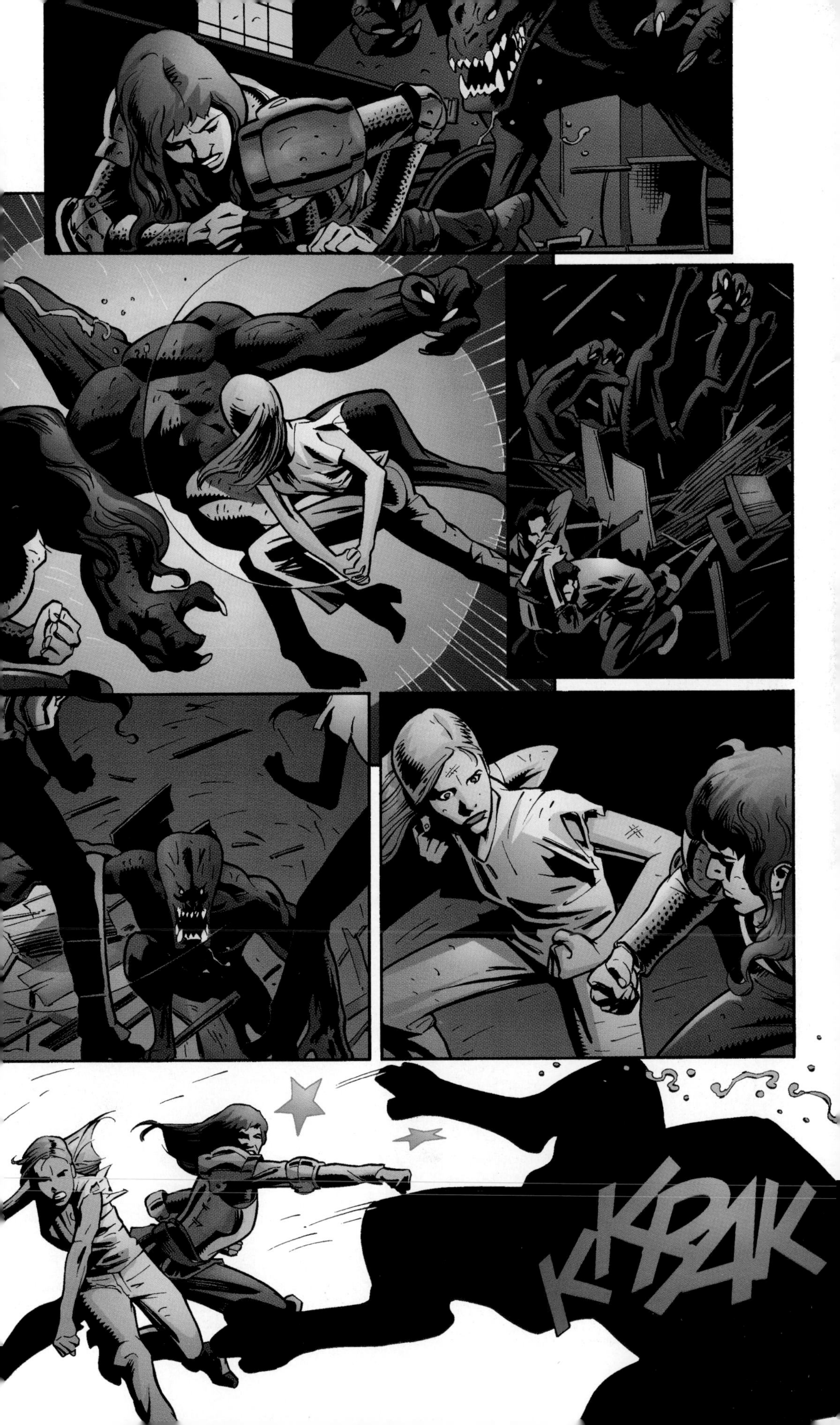
KKRAK

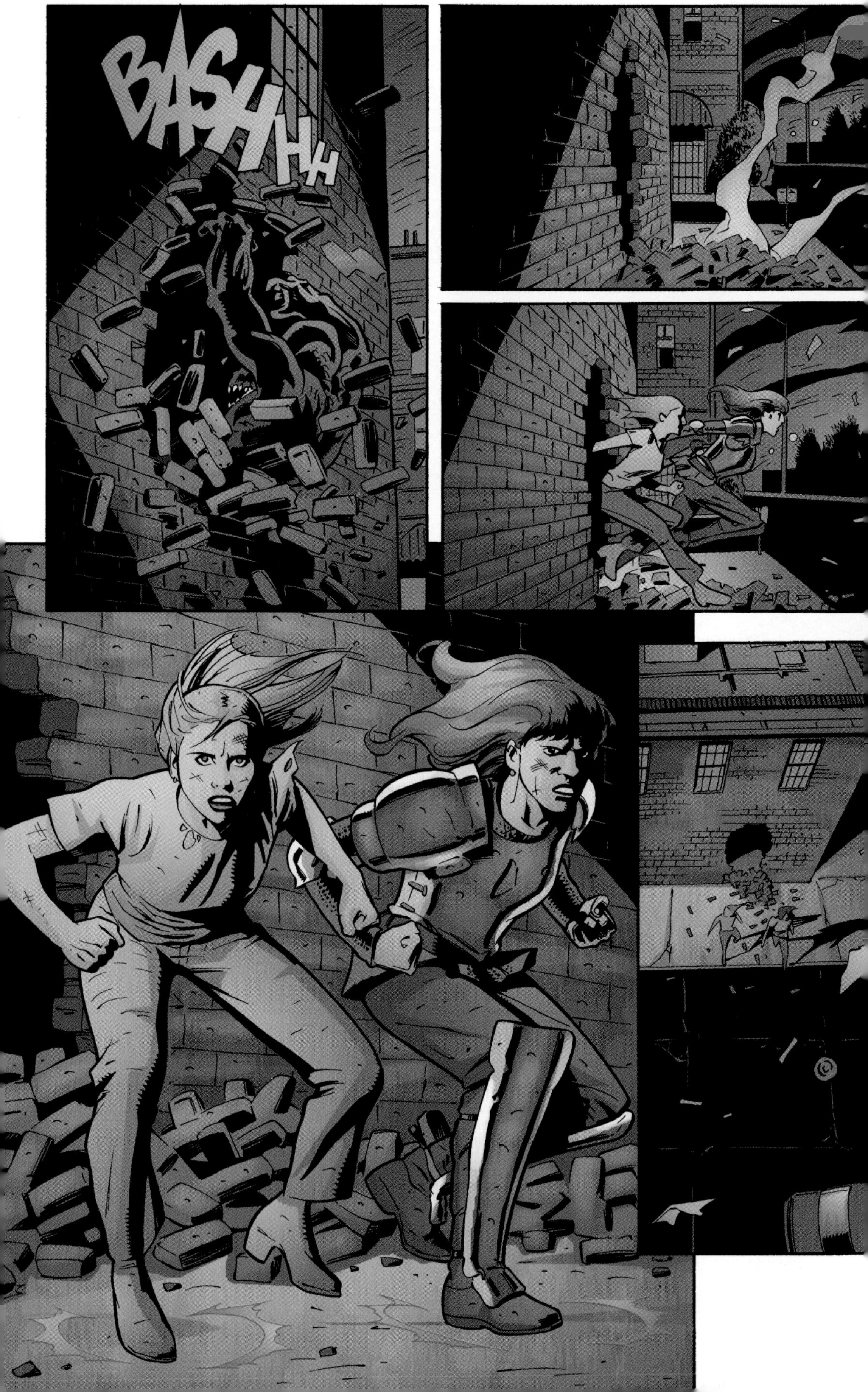
BASHHH

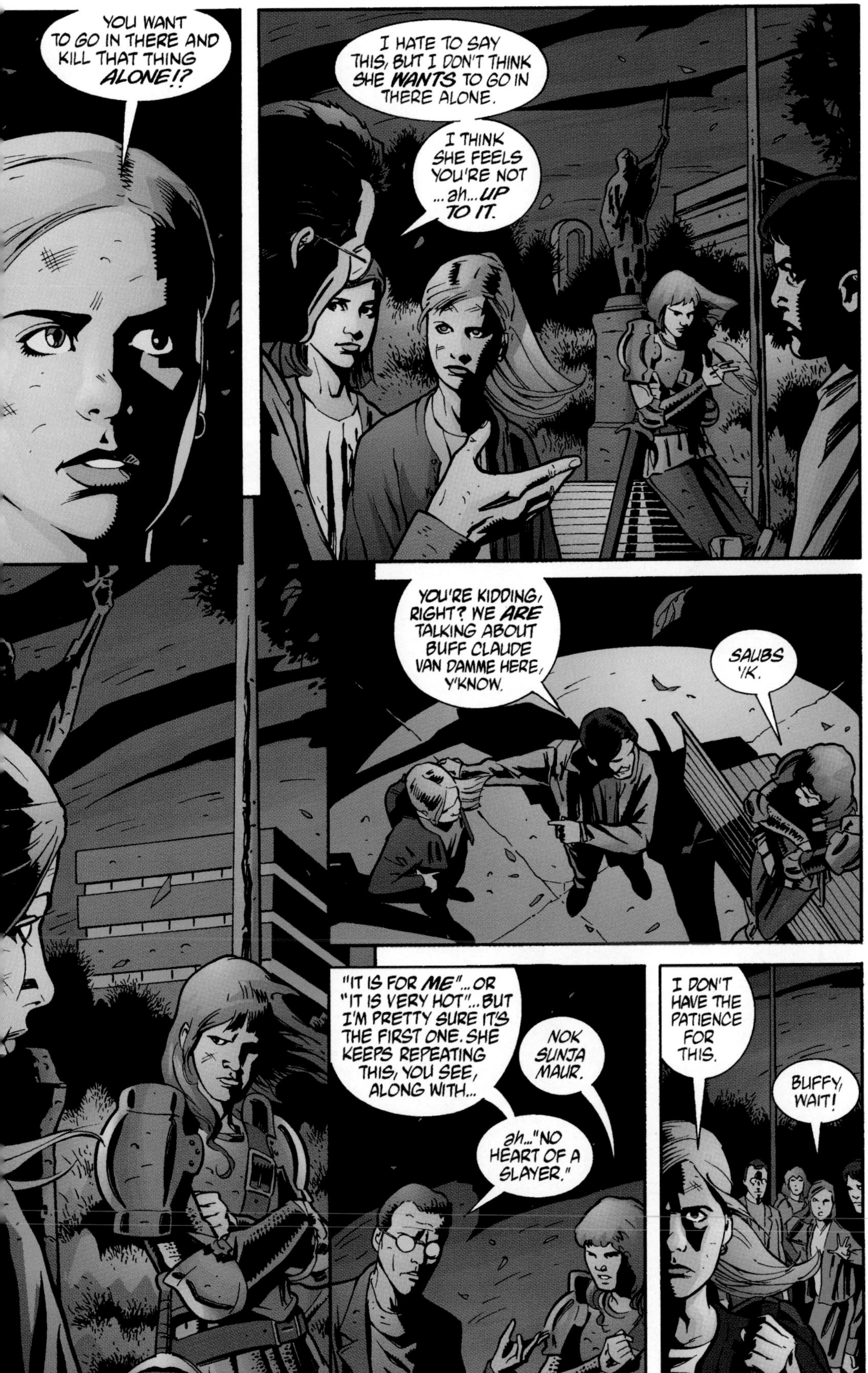
YOU WANT TO GO IN THERE AND KILL THAT THING ALONE!?
I HATE TO SAY THIS, BUT I DON'T THINK SHE WANTS TO GO IN THERE ALONE.
I THINK SHE FEELS YOU'RE NOT ...ah... UP TO IT.
YOU'RE KIDDING, RIGHT? WE ARE TALKING ABOUT BUFF CLAUDE VAN DAMME HERE, Y'KNOW.
SAUBS 'IK.
NOK SUNJA MAUR.
"IT IS FOR ME"...OR "IT IS VERY HOT"...BUT I'M PRETTY SURE IT'S THE FIRST ONE. SHE KEEPS REPEATING THIS, YOU SEE, ALONG WITH...
ah..."NO HEART OF A SLAYER."
I DON'T HAVE THE PATIENCE FOR THIS.
BUFFY, WAIT!

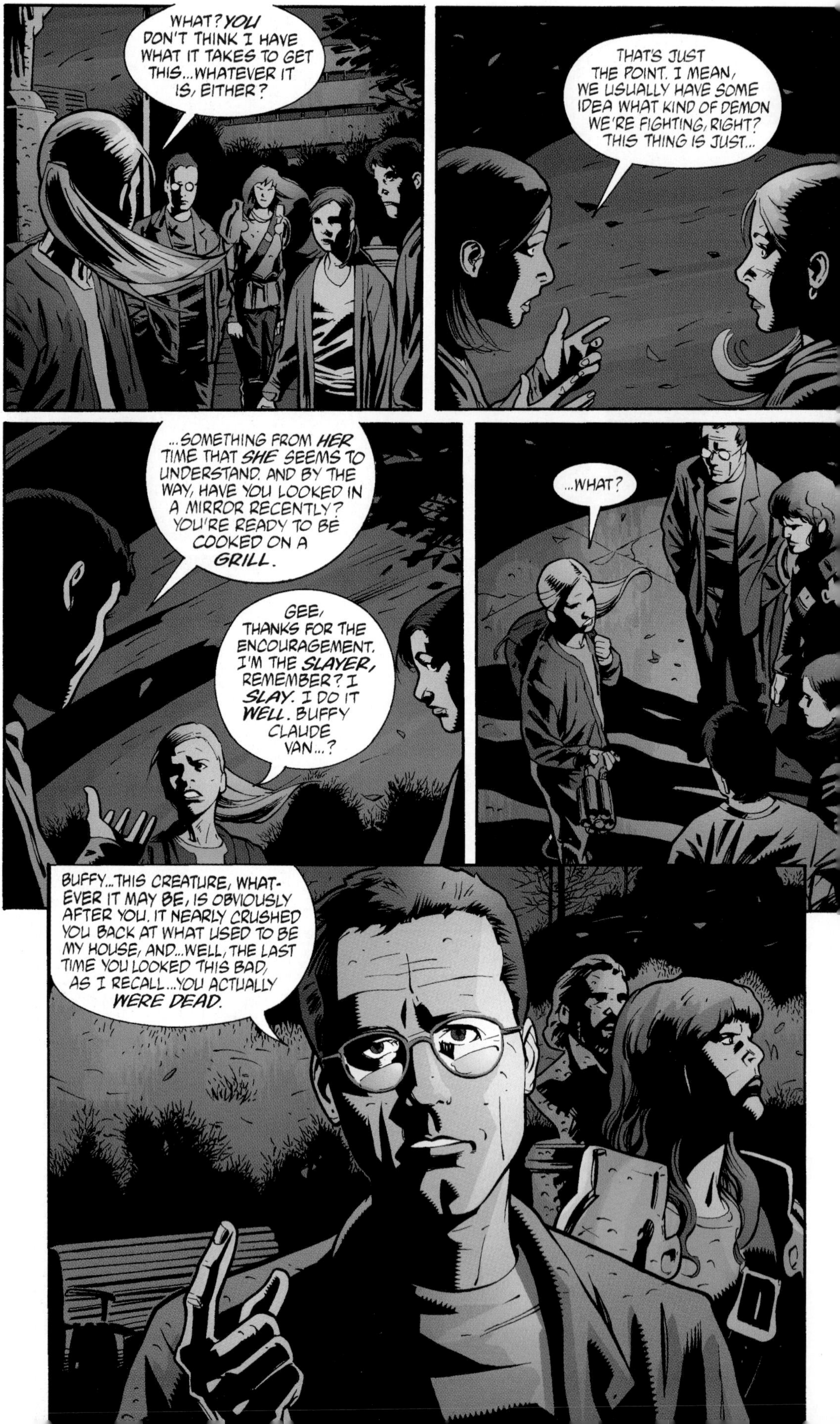
WHAT? YOU DON'T THINK I HAVE WHAT IT TAKES TO GET THIS...WHATEVER IT IS, EITHER?
THAT'S JUST THE POINT. I MEAN, WE USUALLY HAVE SOME IDEA WHAT KIND OF DEMON WE'RE FIGHTING, RIGHT? THIS THING IS JUST...
...SOMETHING FROM HER TIME THAT SHE SEEMS TO UNDERSTAND. AND BY THE WAY, HAVE YOU LOOKED IN A MIRROR RECENTLY? YOU'RE READY TO BE COOKED ON A GRILL.
GEE, THANKS FOR THE ENCOURAGEMENT. I'M THE SLAYER, REMEMBER? I SLAY. I DO IT WELL. BUFFY CLAUDE VAN...?
...WHAT?
BUFFY...THIS CREATURE, WHAT-EVER IT MAY BE, IS OBVIOUSLY AFTER YOU. IT NEARLY CRUSHED YOU BACK AT WHAT USED TO BE MY HOUSE, AND...WELL, THE LAST TIME YOU LOOKED THIS BAD, AS I RECALL...YOU ACTUALLY WERE DEAD.

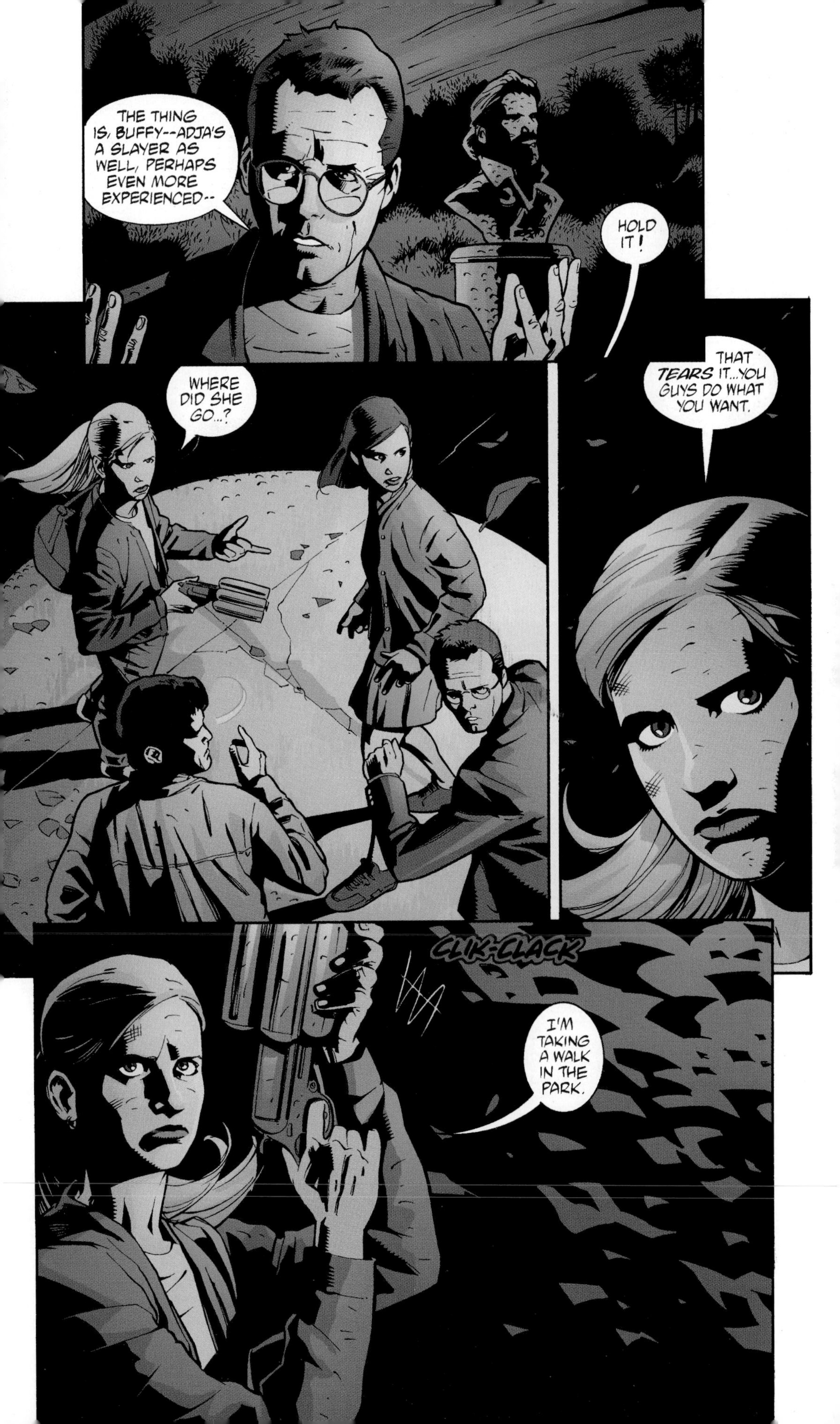
THE THING IS, BUFFY--ADJA'S A SLAYER AS WELL, PERHAPS EVEN MORE EXPERIENCED--
HOLD IT!
WHERE DID SHE GO...?
THAT TEARS IT...YOU GUYS DO WHAT YOU WANT.
CLIK-CLACK
I'M TAKING A WALK IN THE PARK.

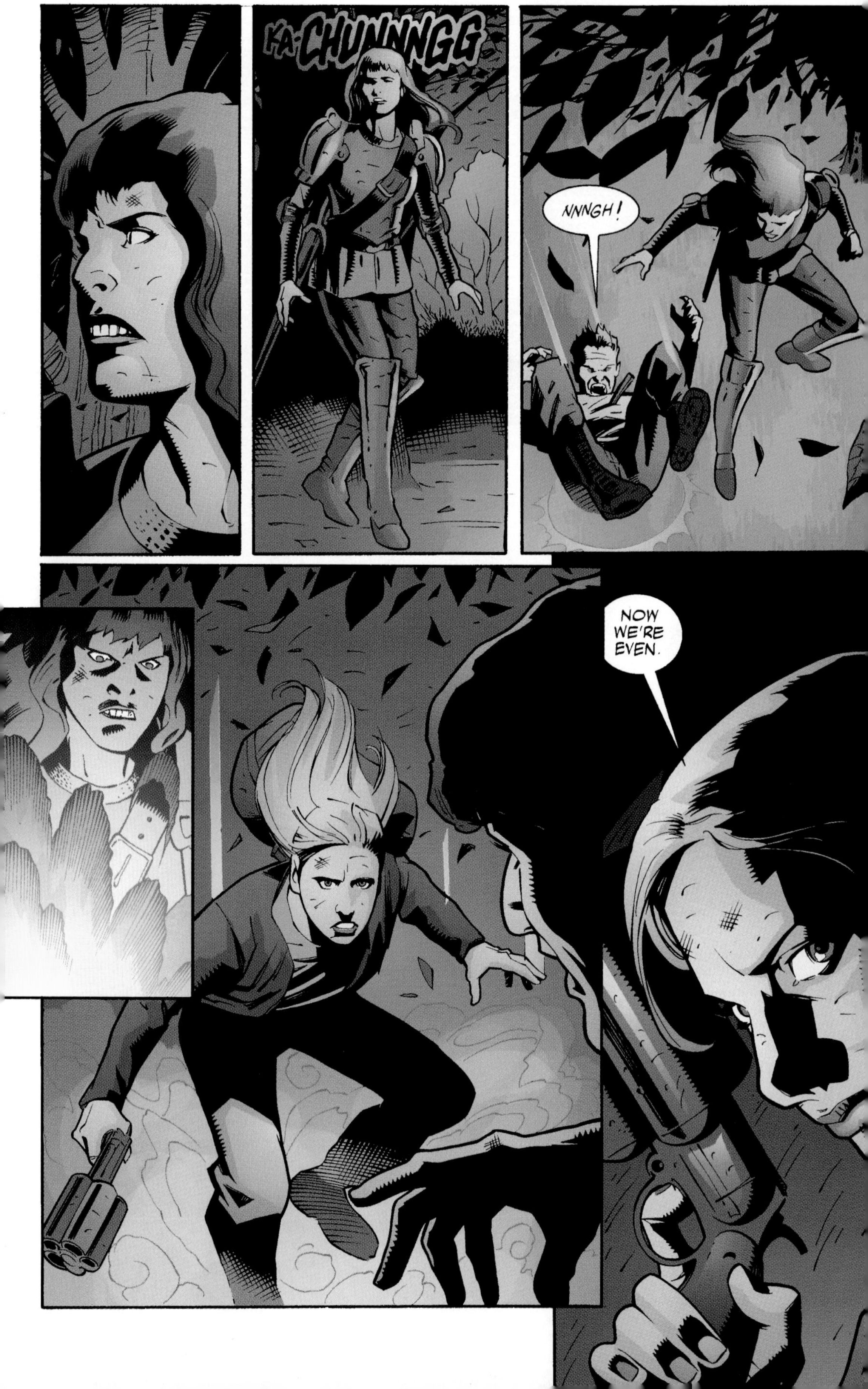
KA-CHUNNNGG
NNNGH!
NOW WE'RE EVEN.

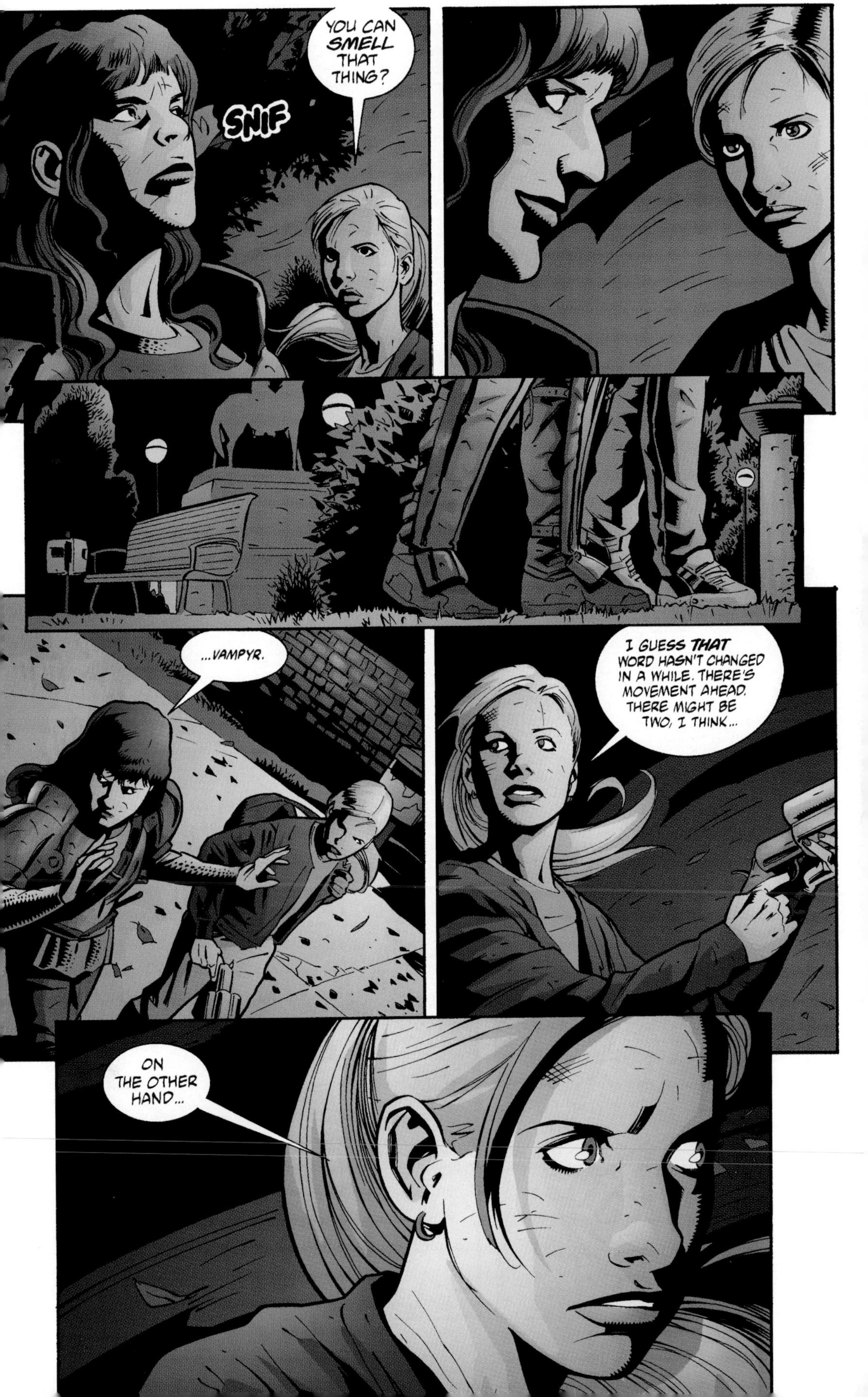
SNIF
YOU CAN SMELL THAT THING?
...VAMPYR.
I GUESS THAT WORD HASN'T CHANGED IN A WHILE. THERE'S MOVEMENT AHEAD. THERE MIGHT BE TWO, I THINK...
ON THE OTHER HAND...

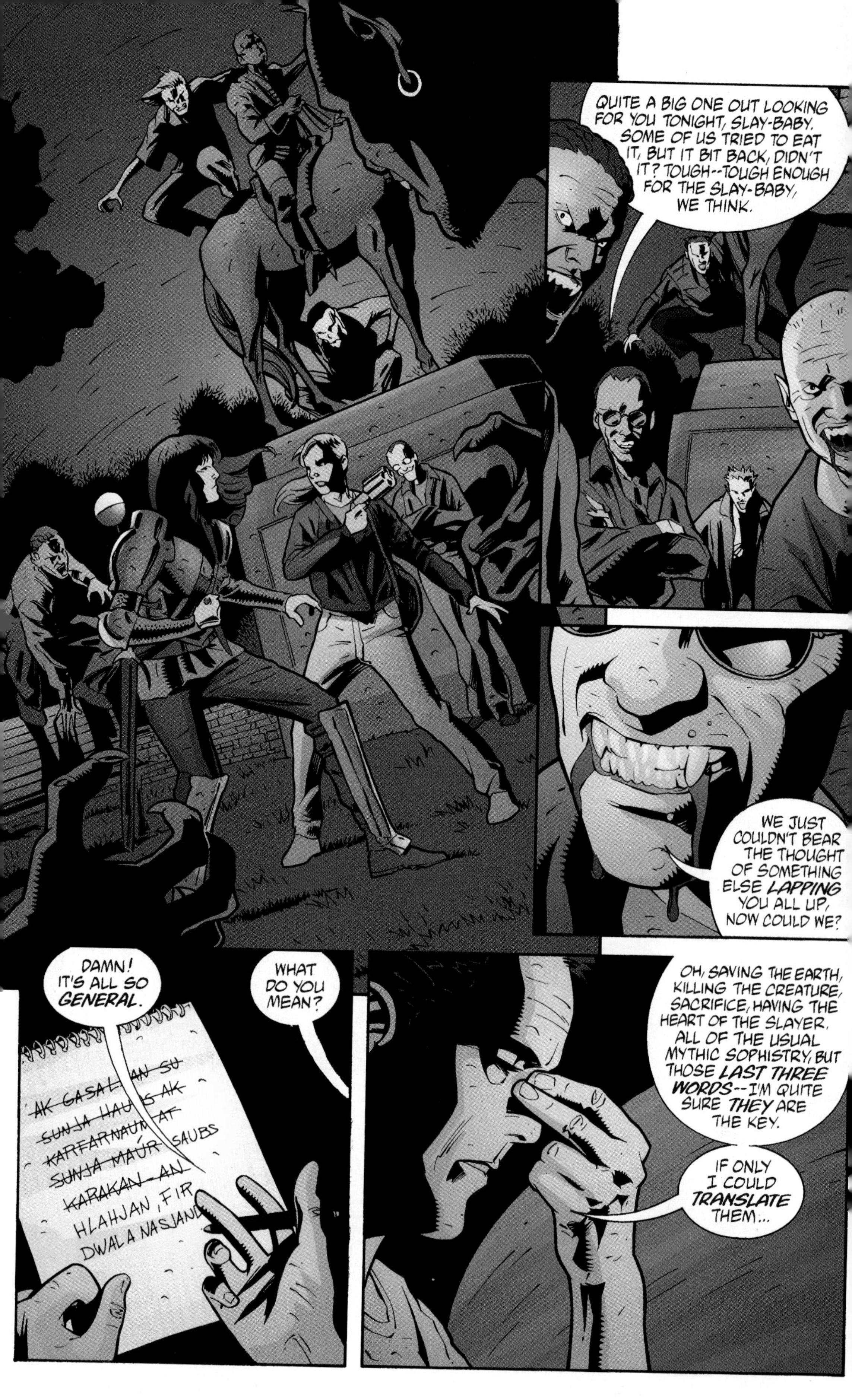

QUITE A BIG ONE OUT LOOKING FOR YOU TONIGHT, SLAY-BABY. SOME OF US TRIED TO EAT IT, BUT IT BIT BACK, DIDN'T IT? TOUGH--TOUGH ENOUGH FOR THE SLAY-BABY, WE THINK.
WE JUST COULDN'T BEAR THE THOUGHT OF SOMETHING ELSE *LAPPING* YOU ALL UP, NOW COULD WE?
DAMN! IT'S ALL SO *GENERAL*.
KARFARNAUM AT
SUNJA MAÚR SAUBS
KARAKAN AN
HLAHJAN, FIR
DWALA NASJAND
WHAT DO YOU MEAN?
OH, SAVING THE EARTH, KILLING THE CREATURE, SACRIFICE, HAVING THE HEART OF THE SLAYER, ALL OF THE USUAL MYTHIC SOPHISTRY, BUT THOSE *LAST THREE WORDS*--I'M QUITE SURE *THEY* ARE THE KEY.
IF ONLY I COULD *TRANSLATE* THEM...

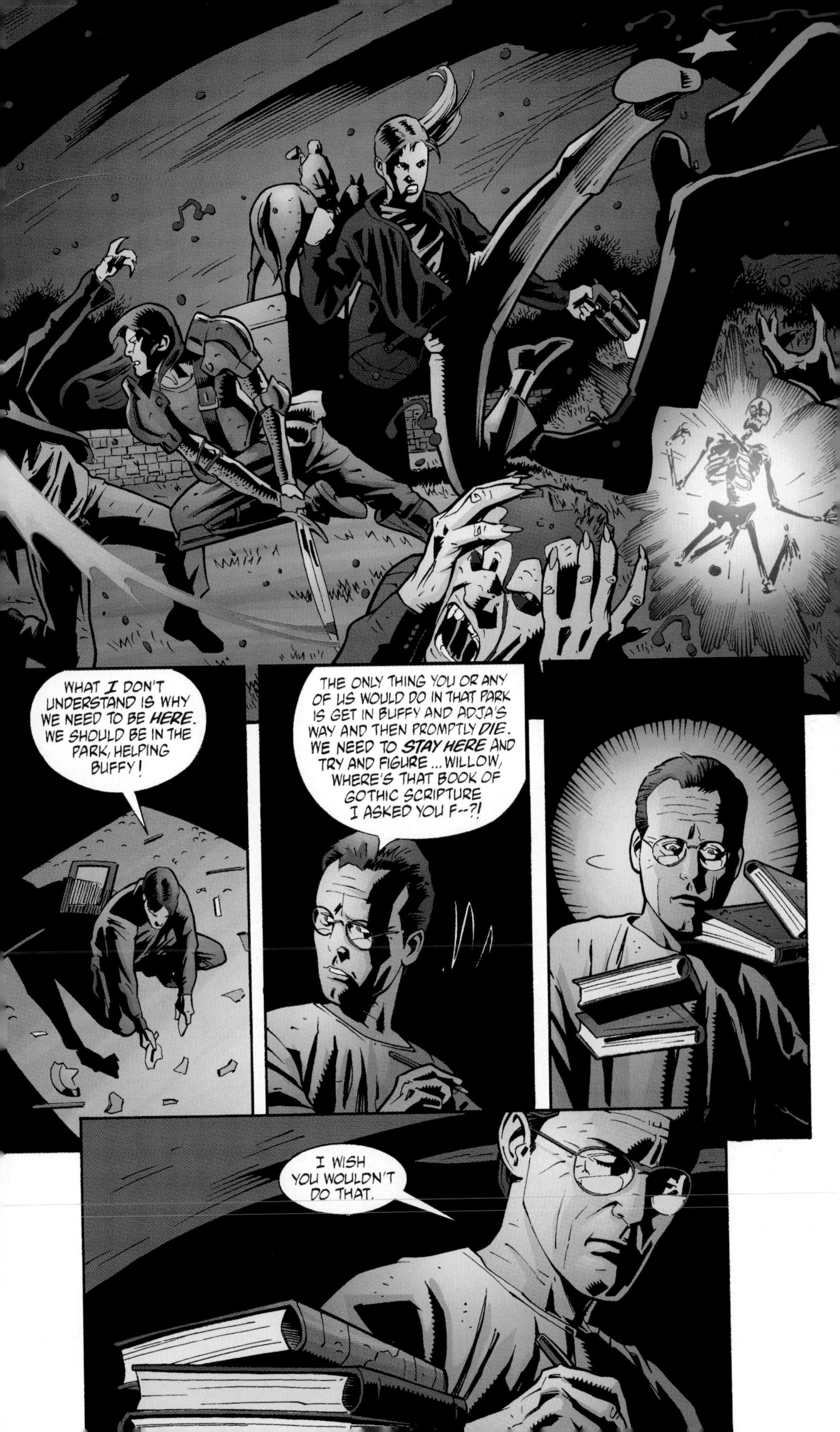
WHAT I DON'T UNDERSTAND IS WHY WE NEED TO BE HERE. WE SHOULD BE IN THE PARK, HELPING BUFFY!
THE ONLY THING YOU OR ANY OF US WOULD DO IN THAT PARK IS GET IN BUFFY AND ADJA'S WAY AND THEN PROMPTLY DIE. WE NEED TO STAY HERE AND TRY AND FIGURE ... WILLOW, WHERE'S THAT BOOK OF GOTHIC SCRIPTURE I ASKED YOU F--?!
I WISH YOU WOULDN'T DO THAT.

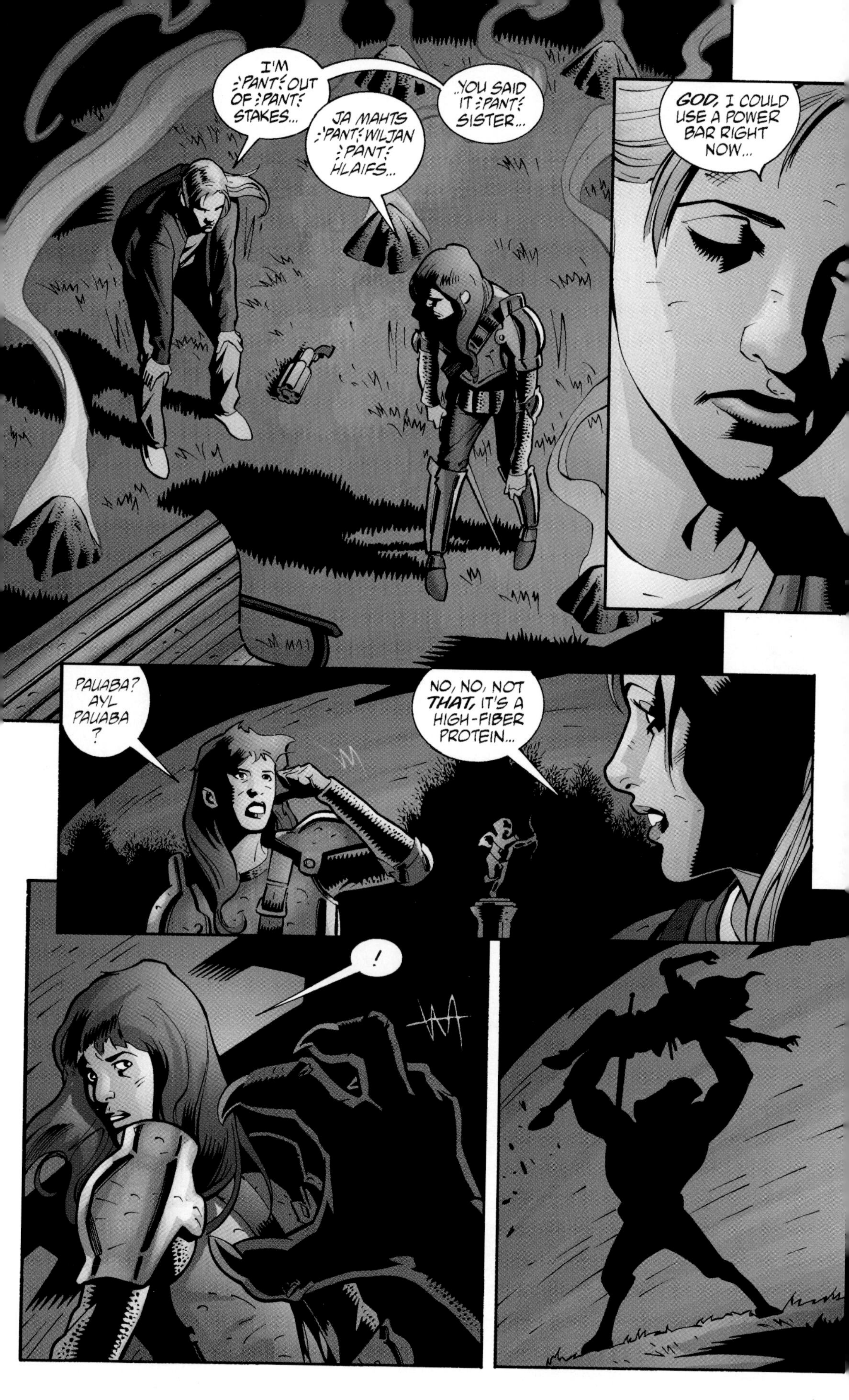
I'M :PANT: OUT OF :PANT: STAKES...
..YOU SAID IT :PANT: SISTER...
JA MAHTS :PANT: WILJAN :PANT: HLAIFS...
GOD, I COULD USE A POWER BAR RIGHT NOW...
PAUABA? AYL PAUABA ?
NO, NO, NOT THAT, IT'S A HIGH-FIBER PROTEIN...
!

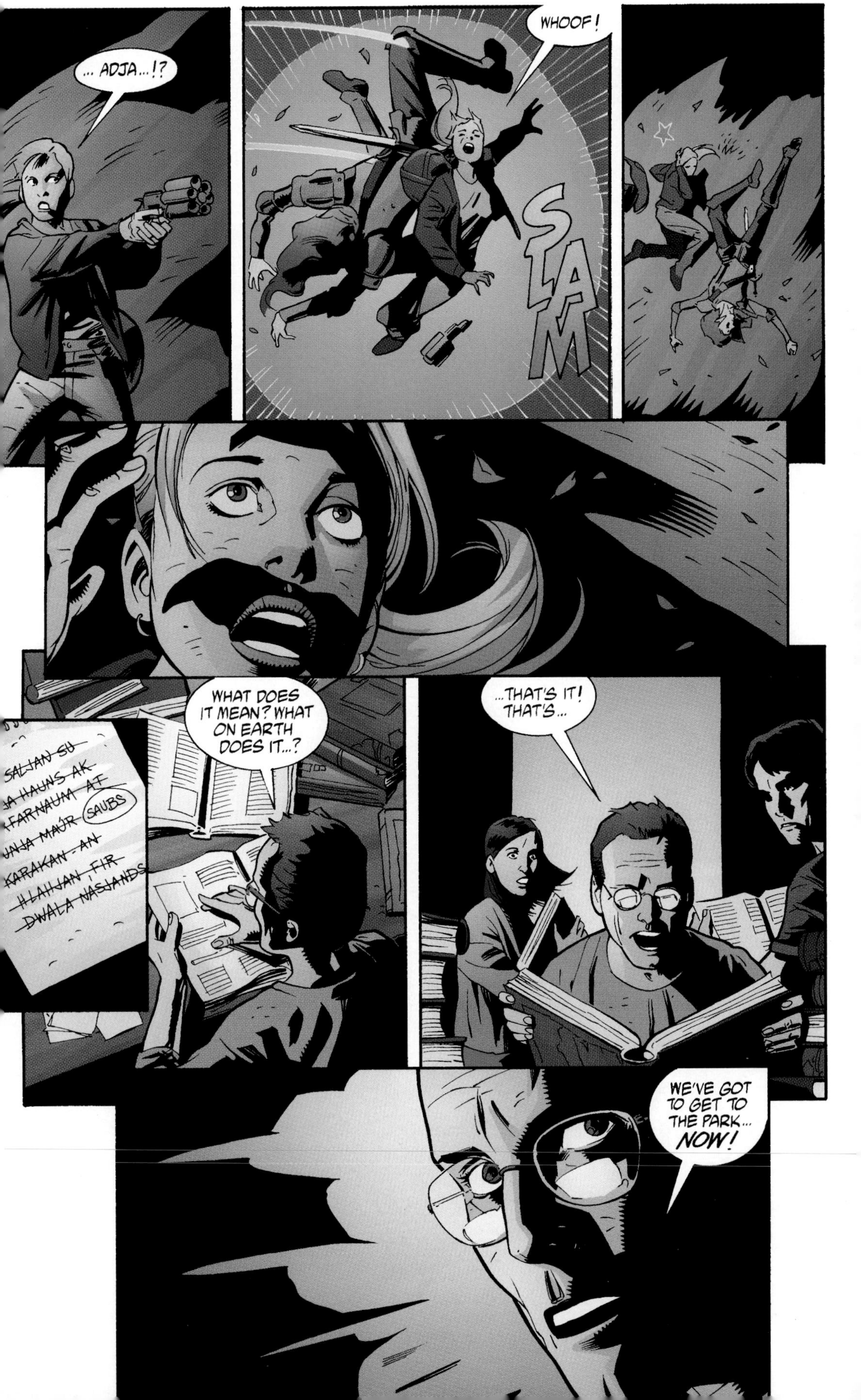
... ADJA...!?
WHOOF!
SLAM
SALJAN SU
JA HAUNS AK
FARNAUM AF
UNJA MAUR SAUBS
KARAKAN AN
ILLAIJAN FIR
DWALA NASJANDS
WHAT DOES IT MEAN? WHAT ON EARTH DOES IT...?
...THAT'S IT! THAT'S...
WE'VE GOT TO GET TO THE PARK... NOW!

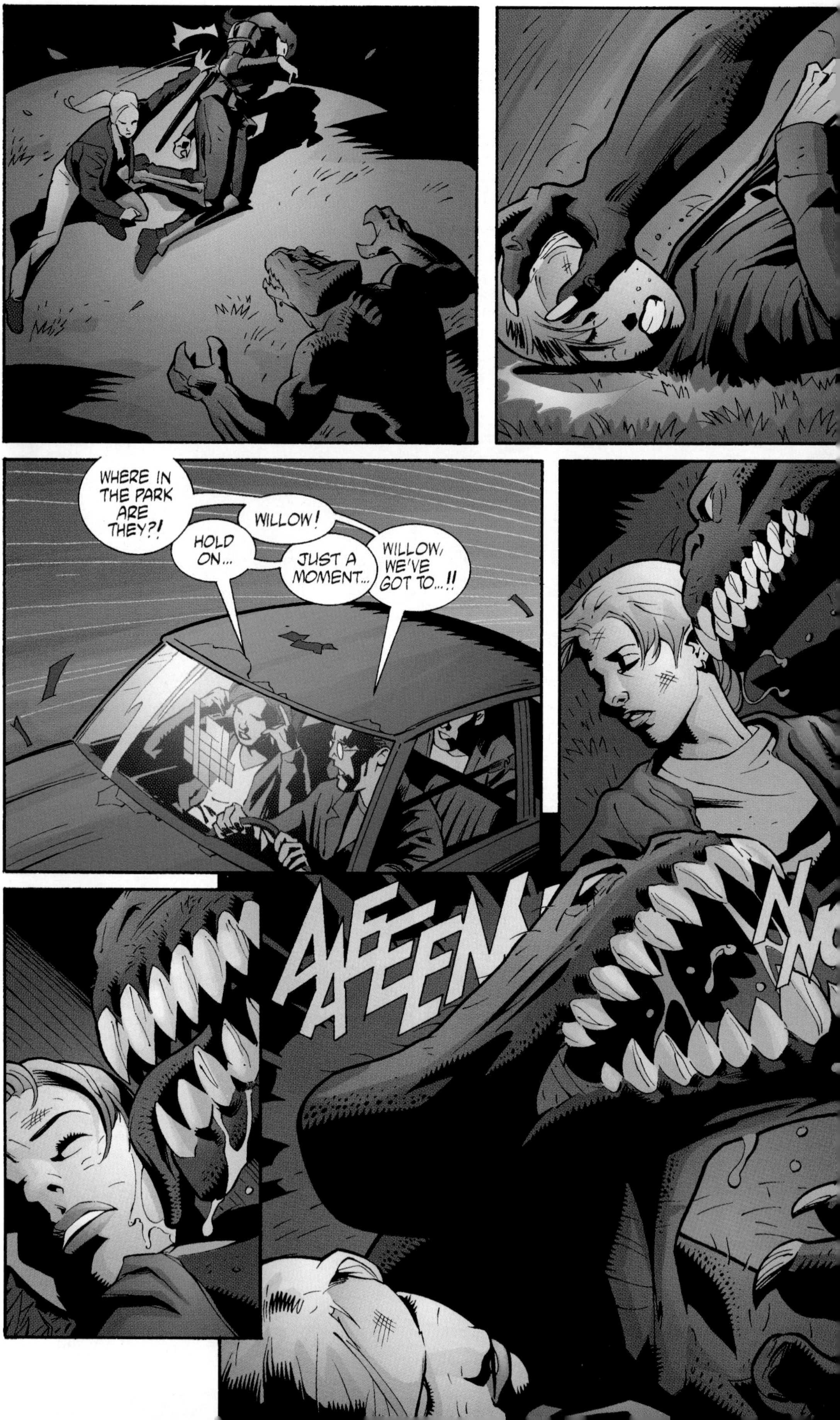
WHERE IN THE PARK ARE THEY?!
WILLOW!
HOLD ON...
JUST A MOMENT...
WILLOW, WE'VE GOT TO...!!

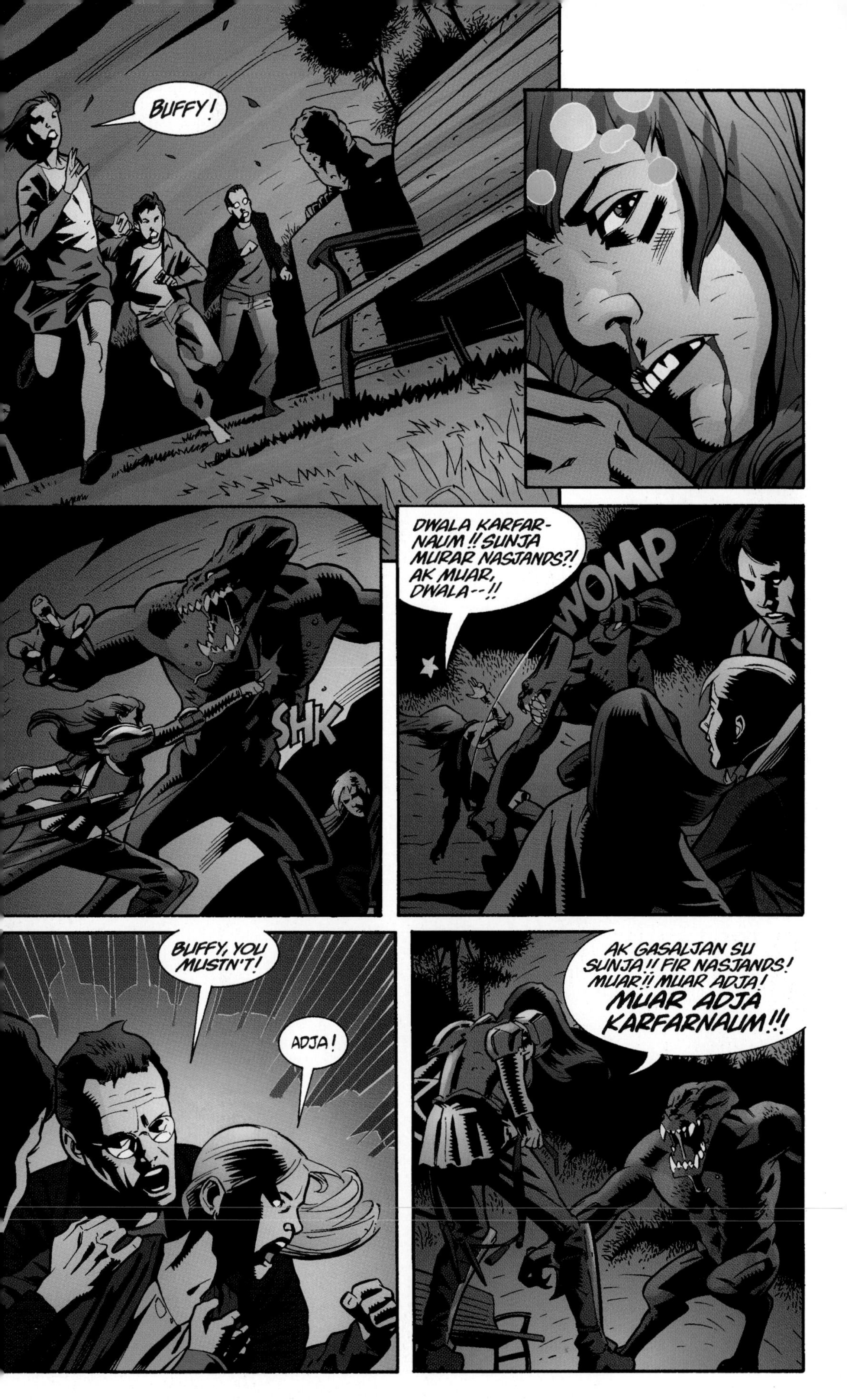
BUFFY!
SHK
DWALA KARFAR-NAUM!! SUNJA MURAR NASJANDS?! AK MUAR, DWALA--!!
WOMP
BUFFY, YOU MUSTN'T!
ADJA!
AK GASALJAN SU SUNJA!! FIR NASJANDS! MUAR!! MUAR ADJA! MUAR ADJA KARFARNAUM!!!

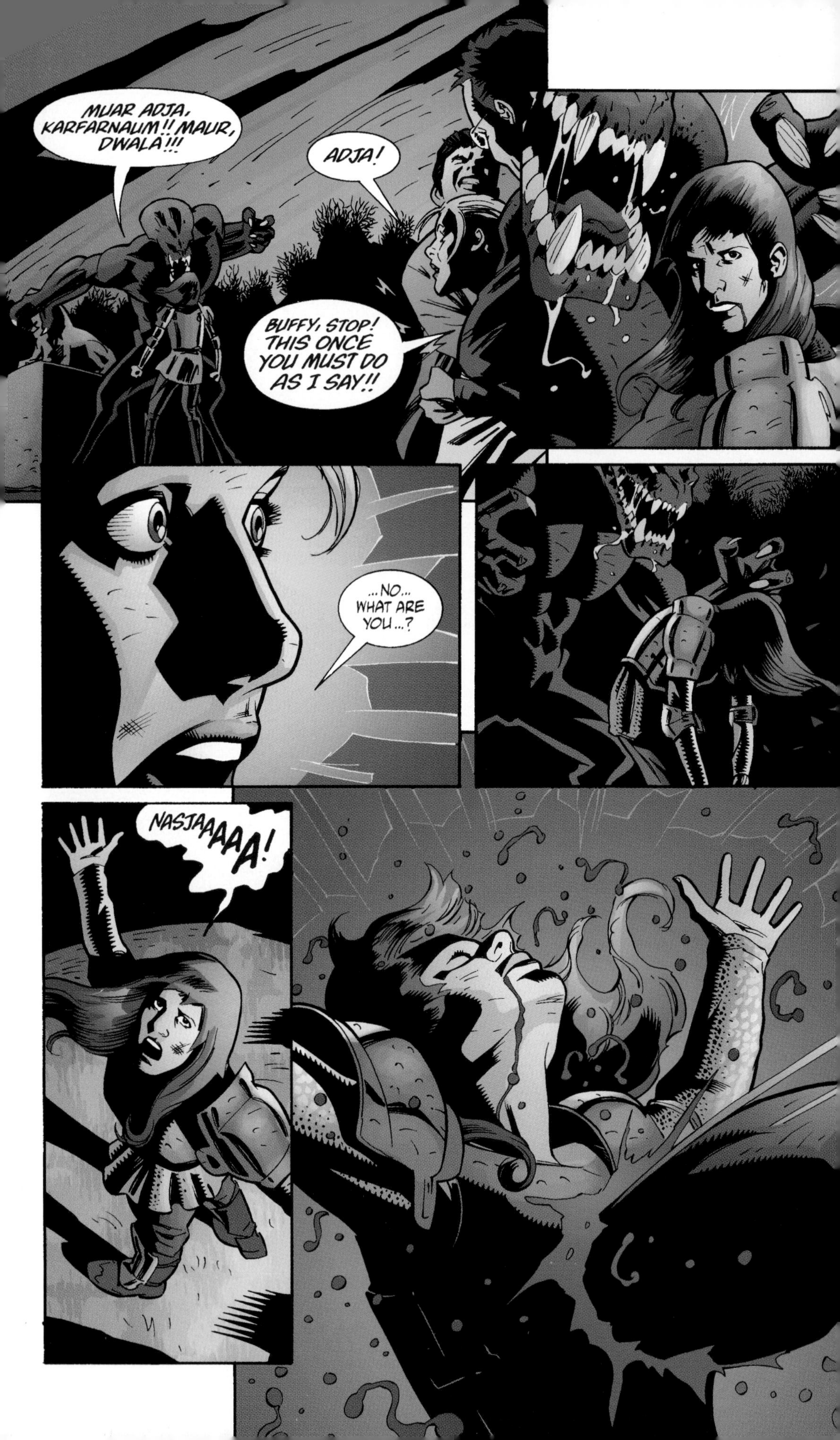

MUAR ADJA, KARFARNAUM!! MAUR, DWALA!!!
ADJA!
BUFFY, STOP! THIS ONCE YOU MUST DO AS I SAY!!
...NO... WHAT ARE YOU...?
NASJAAAAA!

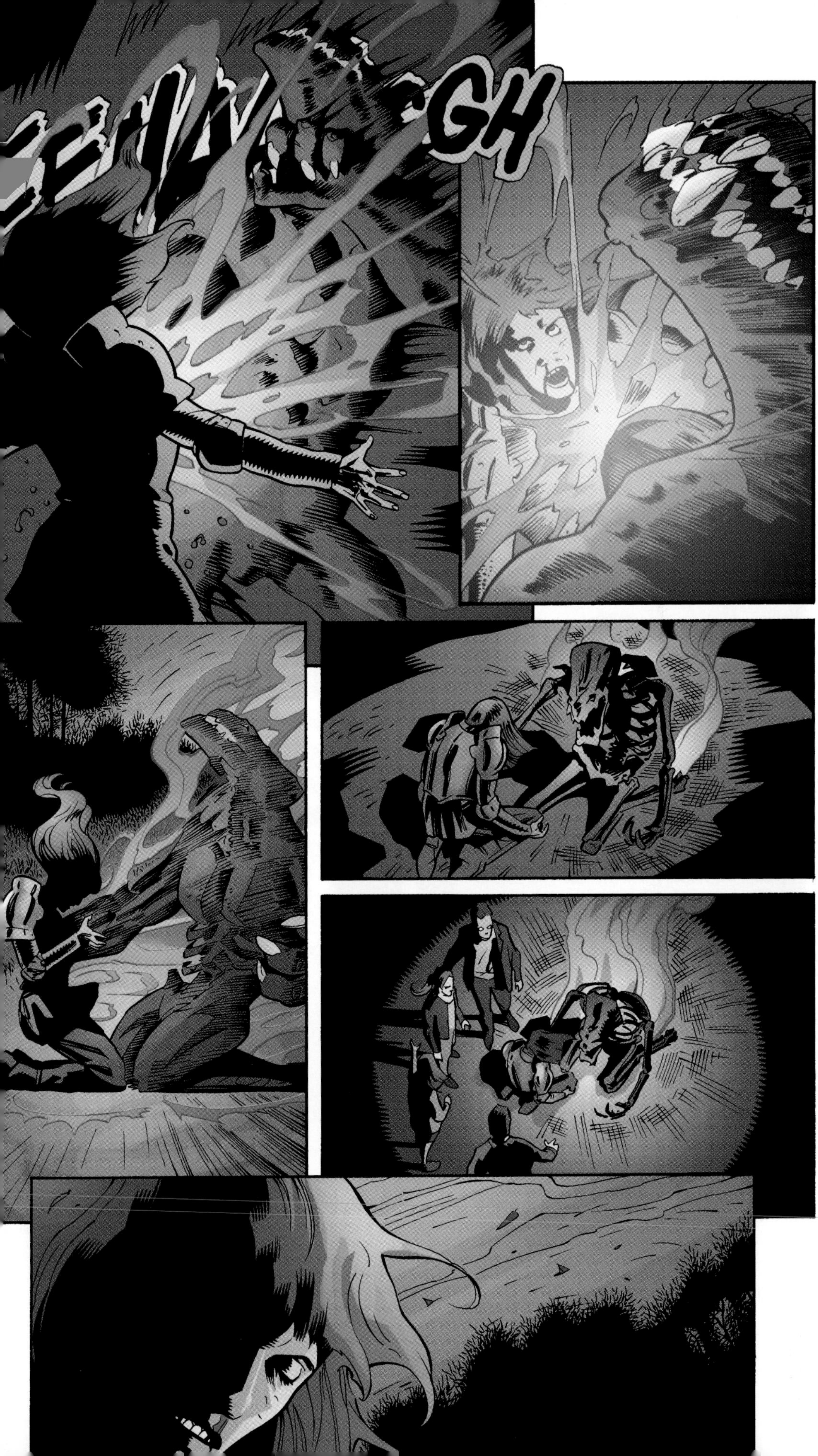
GH

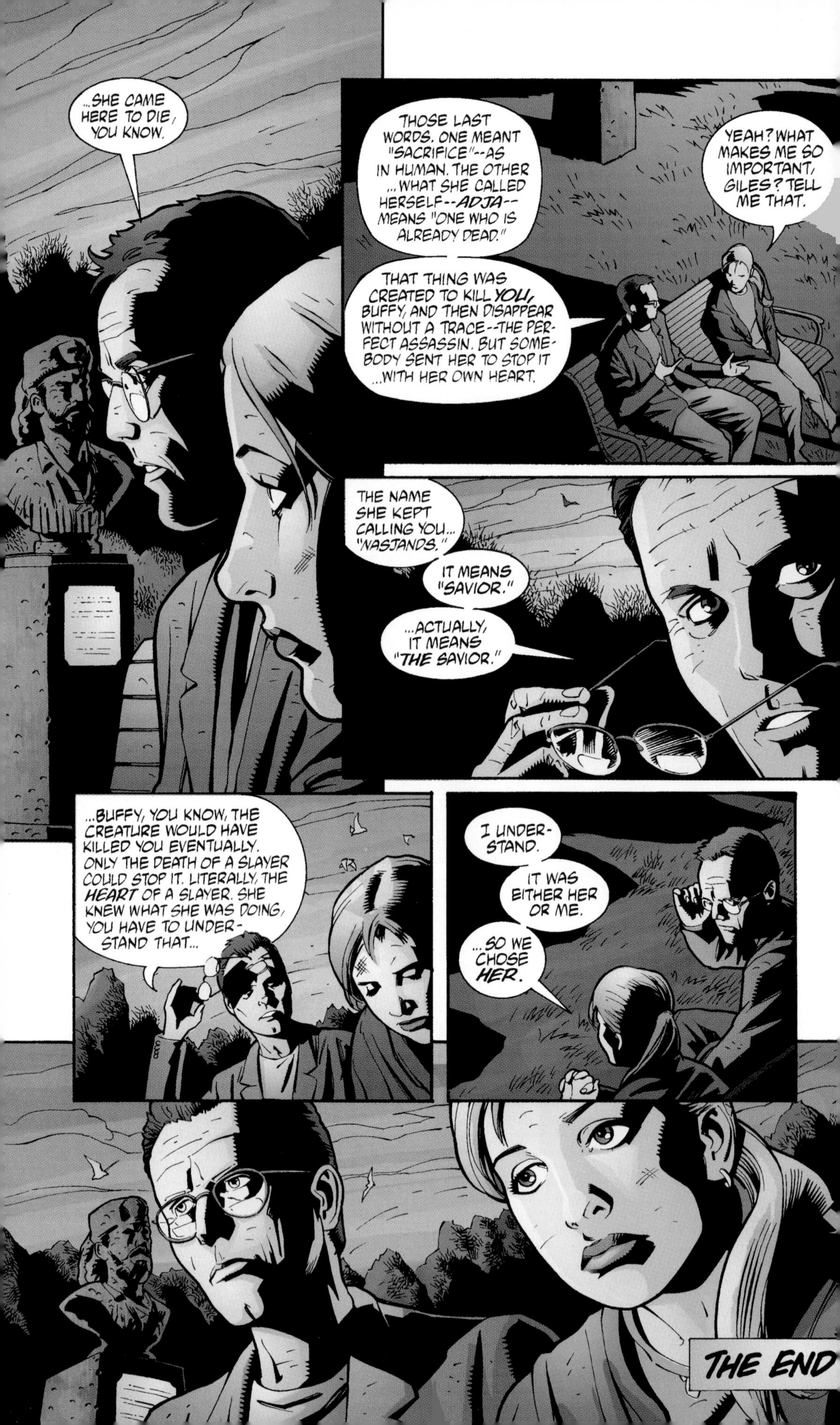
...SHE CAME HERE TO DIE, YOU KNOW.
THOSE LAST WORDS. ONE MEANT "SACRIFICE"--AS IN HUMAN. THE OTHER ...WHAT SHE CALLED HERSELF--ADJA--MEANS "ONE WHO IS ALREADY DEAD."
YEAH? WHAT MAKES ME SO IMPORTANT, GILES? TELL ME THAT.
THAT THING WAS CREATED TO KILL YOU, BUFFY, AND THEN DISAPPEAR WITHOUT A TRACE--THE PERFECT ASSASSIN. BUT SOMEBODY SENT HER TO STOP IT ...WITH HER OWN HEART.
THE NAME SHE KEPT CALLING YOU... "NASJANDS."
IT MEANS "SAVIOR."
...ACTUALLY, IT MEANS "THE SAVIOR."
...BUFFY, YOU KNOW, THE CREATURE WOULD HAVE KILLED YOU EVENTUALLY. ONLY THE DEATH OF A SLAYER COULD STOP IT. LITERALLY, THE HEART OF A SLAYER. SHE KNEW WHAT SHE WAS DOING, YOU HAVE TO UNDERSTAND THAT...
I UNDERSTAND.
IT WAS EITHER HER OR ME.
...SO WE CHOSE HER.
THE END

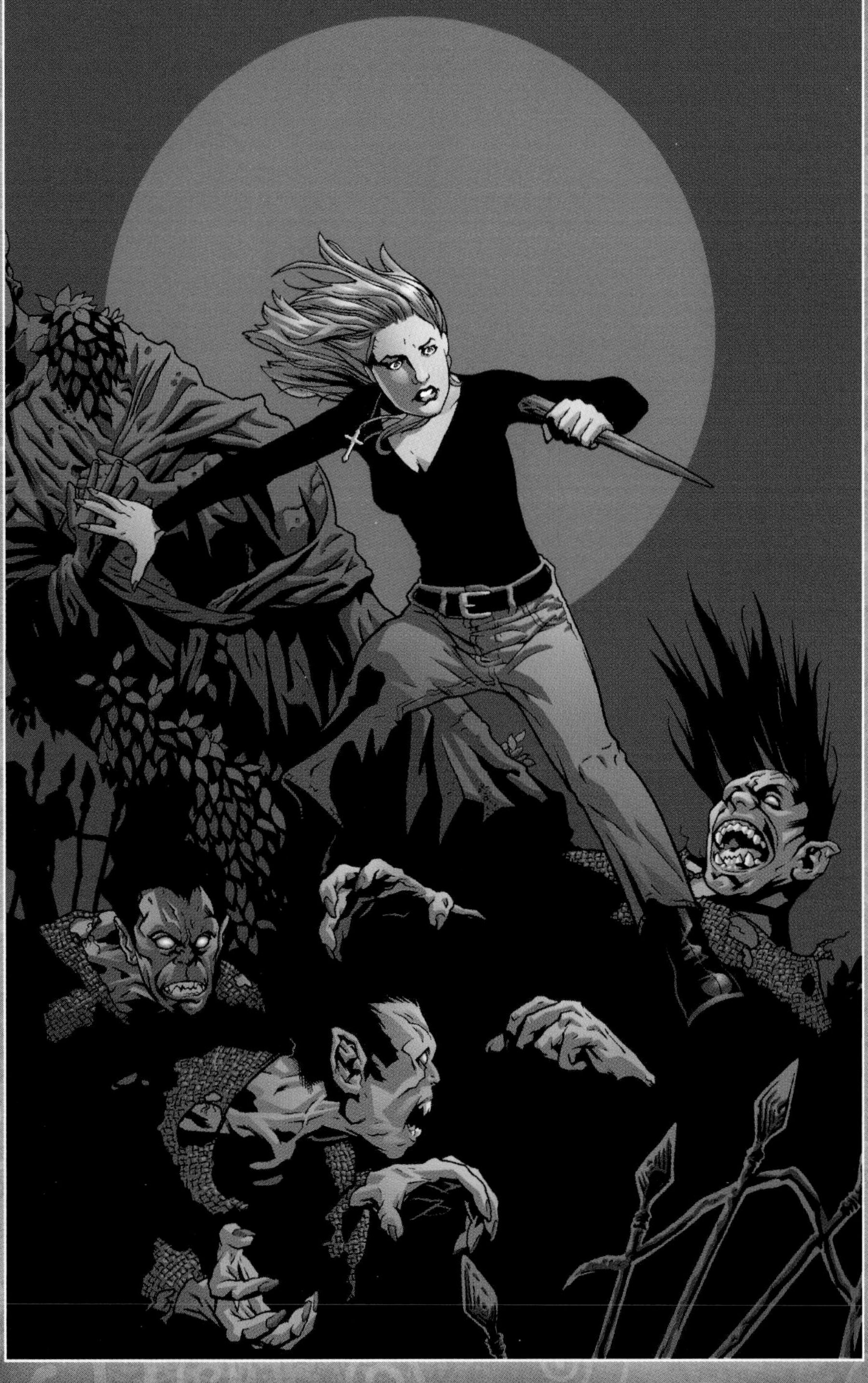

Art by RYAN SOOK *and* GALEN SHOWMAN
with DAVE STEWART

CEMETERY
OF
LOST LOVE

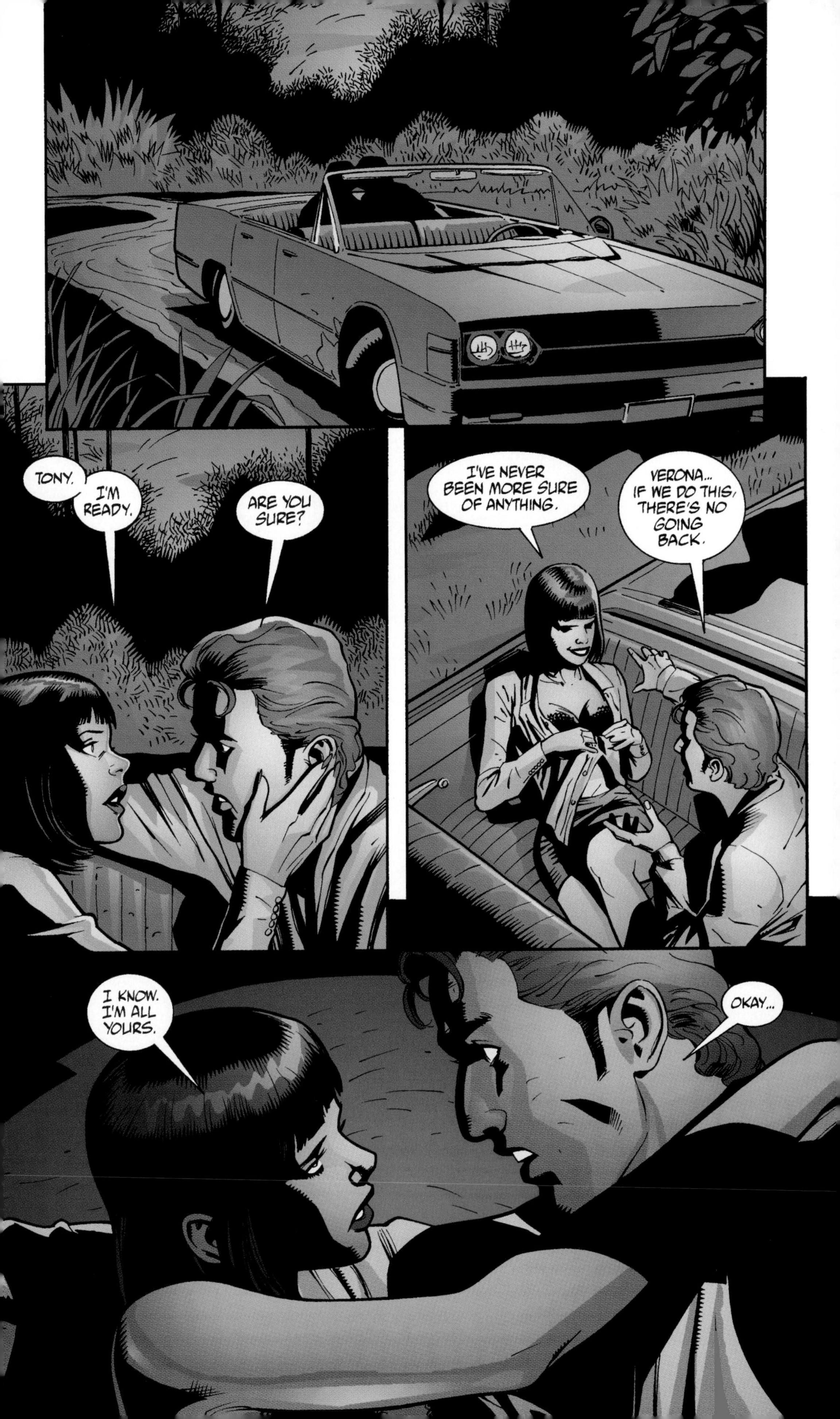
TONY.
I'M READY.
ARE YOU SURE?
I'VE NEVER BEEN MORE SURE OF ANYTHING.
VERONA... IF WE DO THIS, THERE'S NO GOING BACK.
I KNOW. I'M ALL YOURS.
OKAY...

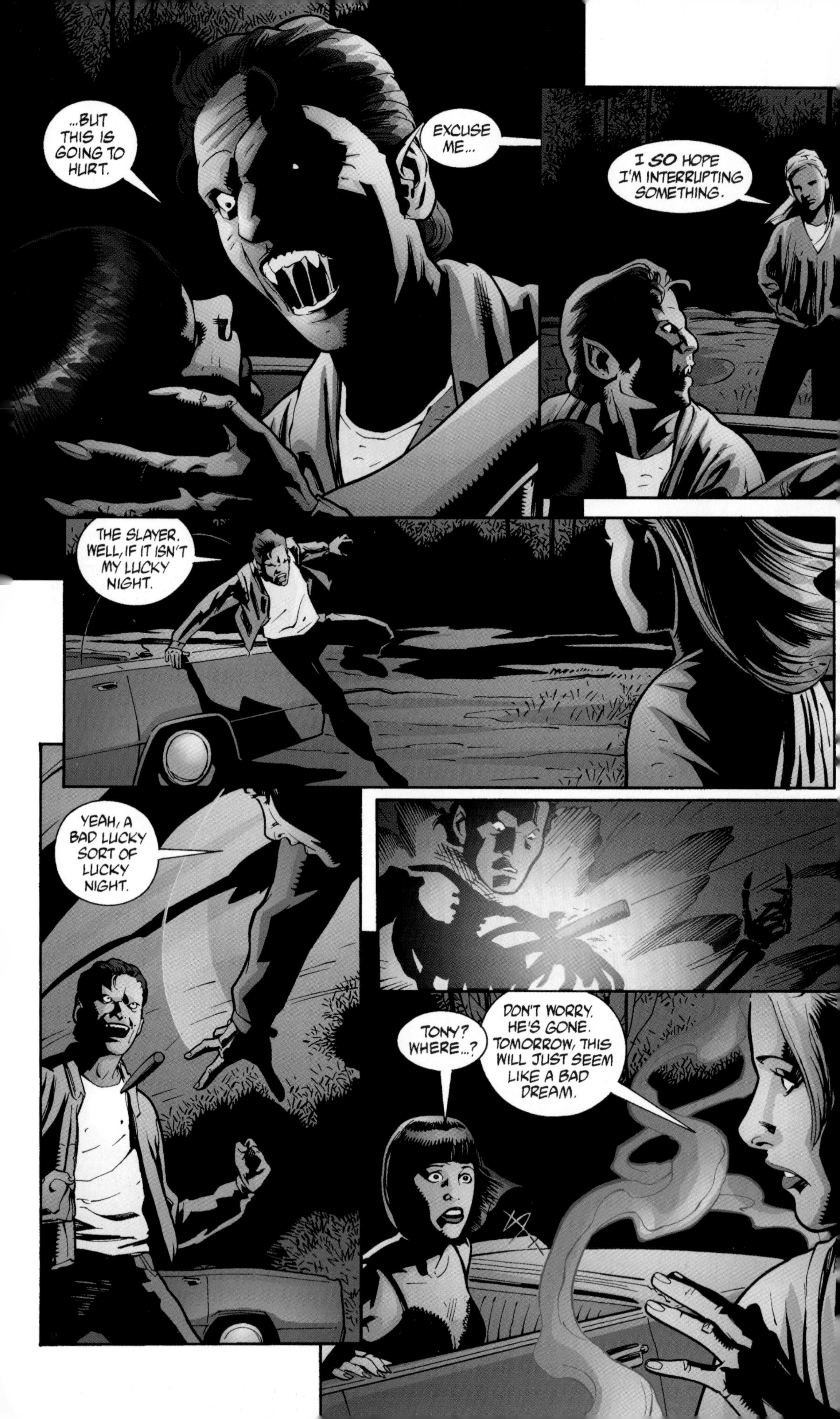
...BUT THIS IS GOING TO HURT.
EXCUSE ME...
I SO HOPE I'M INTERRUPTING SOMETHING.
THE SLAYER. WELL, IF IT ISN'T MY LUCKY NIGHT.
YEAH, A BAD LUCKY SORT OF LUCKY NIGHT.
TONY? WHERE...?
DON'T WORRY. HE'S GONE. TOMORROW, THIS WILL JUST SEEM LIKE A BAD DREAM.

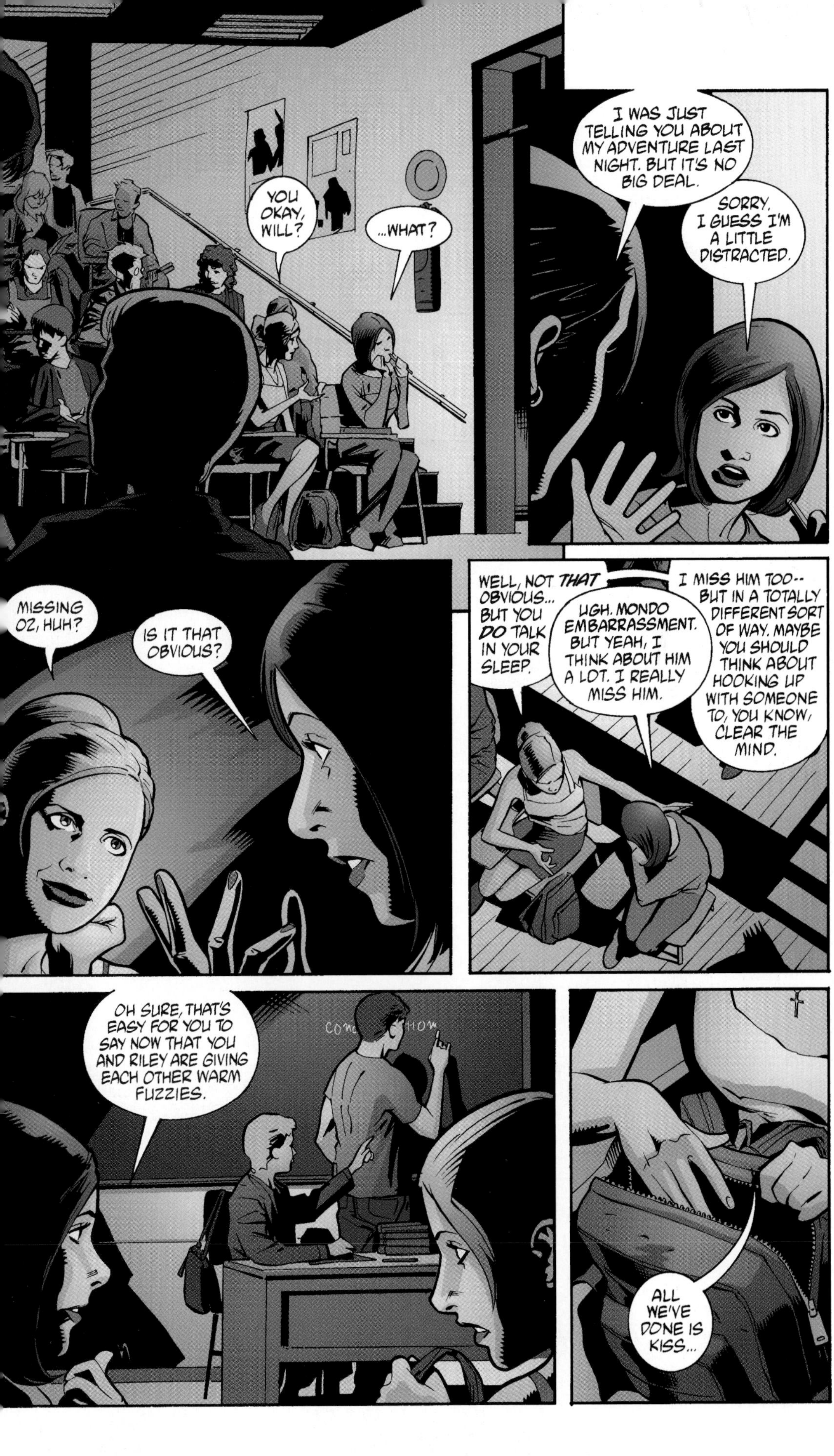
YOU OKAY, WILL?
...WHAT?
I WAS JUST TELLING YOU ABOUT MY ADVENTURE LAST NIGHT. BUT IT'S NO BIG DEAL.
SORRY, I GUESS I'M A LITTLE DISTRACTED.
MISSING OZ, HUH?
IS IT THAT OBVIOUS?
WELL, NOT THAT OBVIOUS... BUT YOU DO TALK IN YOUR SLEEP.
UGH. MONDO EMBARRASSMENT. BUT YEAH, I THINK ABOUT HIM A LOT. I REALLY MISS HIM.
I MISS HIM TOO-- BUT IN A TOTALLY DIFFERENT SORT OF WAY. MAYBE YOU SHOULD THINK ABOUT HOOKING UP WITH SOMEONE TO, YOU KNOW, CLEAR THE MIND.
OH SURE, THAT'S EASY FOR YOU TO SAY NOW THAT YOU AND RILEY ARE GIVING EACH OTHER WARM FUZZIES.
ALL WE'VE DONE IS KISS...

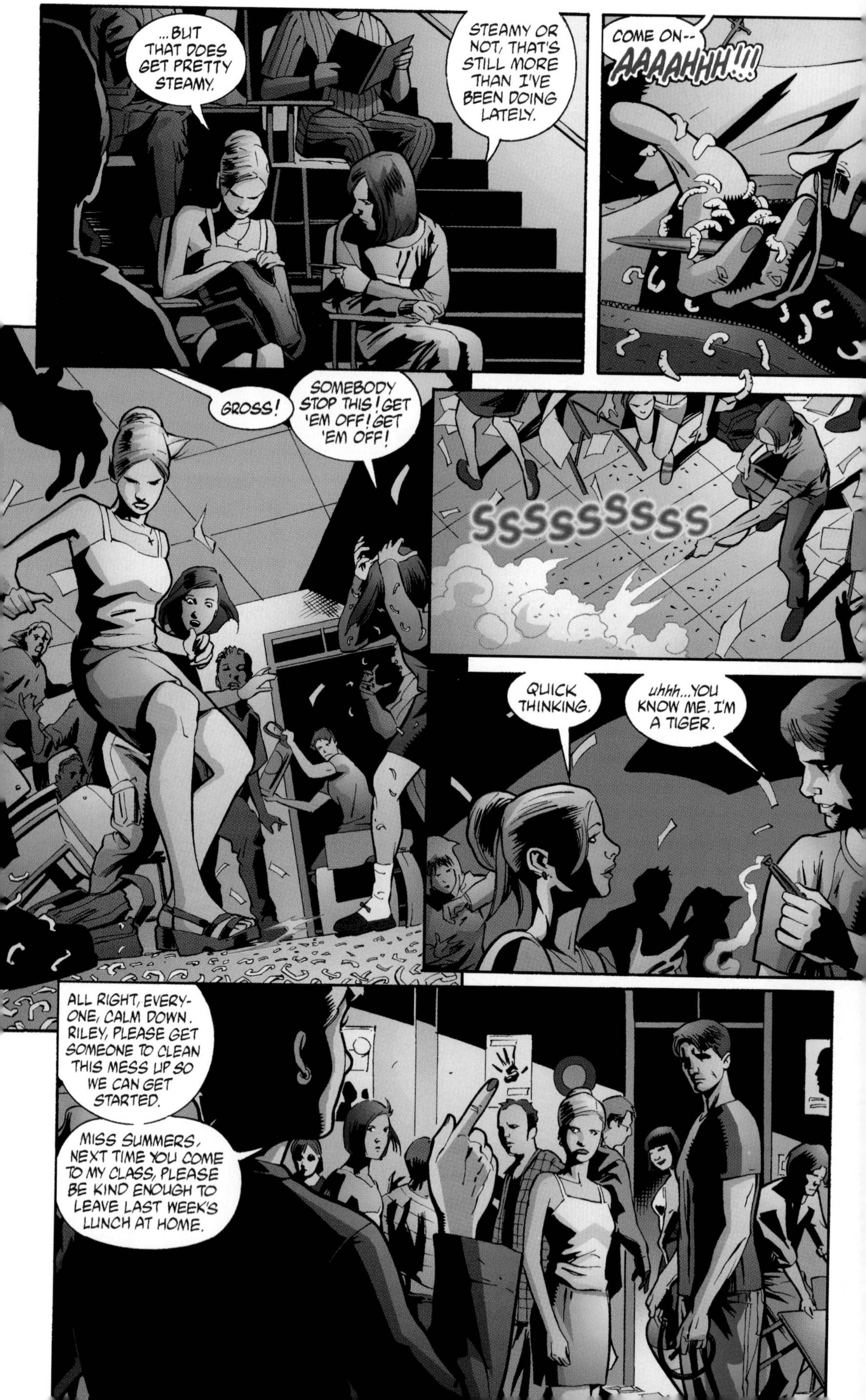
...BUT THAT DOES GET PRETTY STEAMY.
STEAMY OR NOT, THAT'S STILL MORE THAN I'VE BEEN DOING LATELY.
COME ON--
AAAAHHH!!!
GROSS!
SOMEBODY STOP THIS! GET 'EM OFF! GET 'EM OFF!
SSSSSSSSSS
QUICK THINKING.
uhhh...YOU KNOW ME. I'M A TIGER.
ALL RIGHT, EVERY-ONE, CALM DOWN. RILEY, PLEASE GET SOMEONE TO CLEAN THIS MESS UP SO WE CAN GET STARTED.
MISS SUMMERS, NEXT TIME YOU COME TO MY CLASS, PLEASE BE KIND ENOUGH TO LEAVE LAST WEEK'S LUNCH AT HOME.

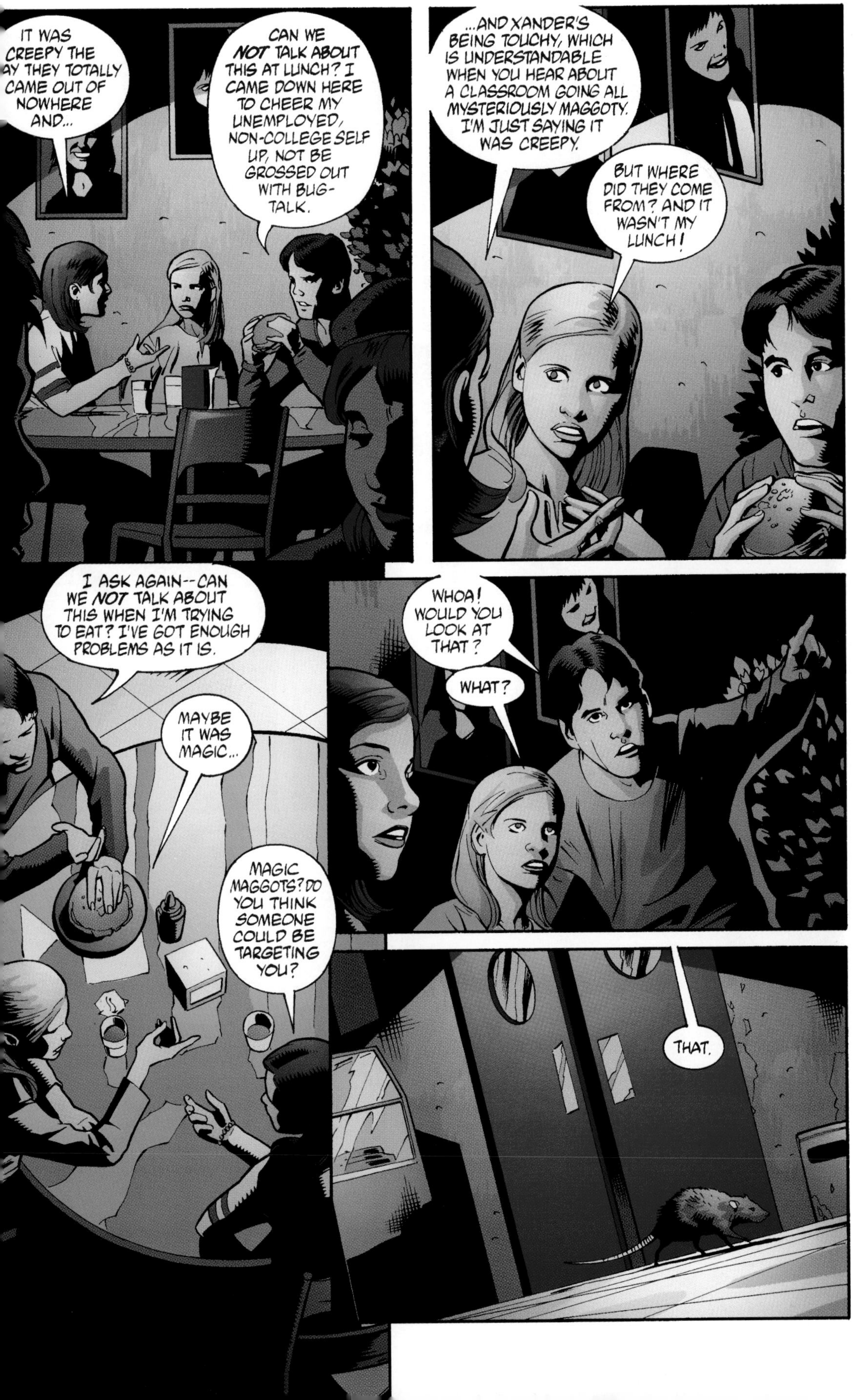
IT WAS CREEPY THE AY THEY TOTALLY CAME OUT OF NOWHERE AND...
CAN WE NOT TALK ABOUT THIS AT LUNCH? I CAME DOWN HERE TO CHEER MY UNEMPLOYED, NON-COLLEGE SELF UP, NOT BE GROSSED OUT WITH BUG-TALK.
...AND XANDER'S BEING TOUCHY, WHICH IS UNDERSTANDABLE WHEN YOU HEAR ABOUT A CLASSROOM GOING ALL MYSTERIOUSLY MAGGOTY. I'M JUST SAYING IT WAS CREEPY.
BUT WHERE DID THEY COME FROM? AND IT WASN'T MY LUNCH!
I ASK AGAIN--CAN WE NOT TALK ABOUT THIS WHEN I'M TRYING TO EAT? I'VE GOT ENOUGH PROBLEMS AS IT IS.
MAYBE IT WAS MAGIC...
MAGIC MAGGOTS? DO YOU THINK SOMEONE COULD BE TARGETING YOU?
WHOA! WOULD YOU LOOK AT THAT?
WHAT?
THAT.

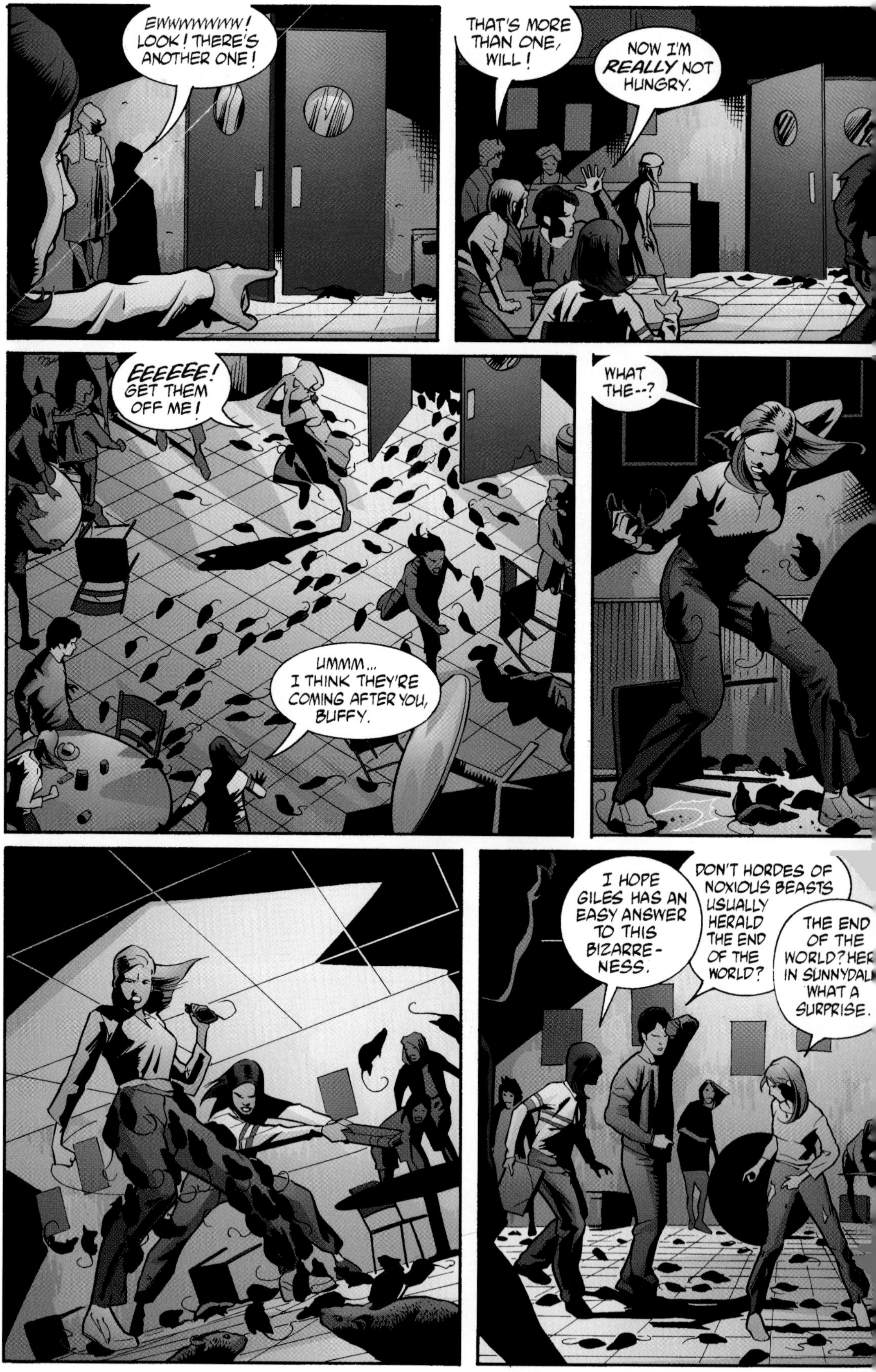

EWWWWWWW! LOOK! THERE'S ANOTHER ONE!
THAT'S MORE THAN ONE, WILL!
NOW I'M REALLY NOT HUNGRY.
EEEEEE! GET THEM OFF ME!
UMMM... I THINK THEY'RE COMING AFTER YOU, BUFFY.
WHAT THE--?
I HOPE GILES HAS AN EASY ANSWER TO THIS BIZARRE-NESS.
DON'T HORDES OF NOXIOUS BEASTS USUALLY HERALD THE END OF THE WORLD?
THE END OF THE WORLD? HER IN SUNNYDAL WHAT A SURPRISE.

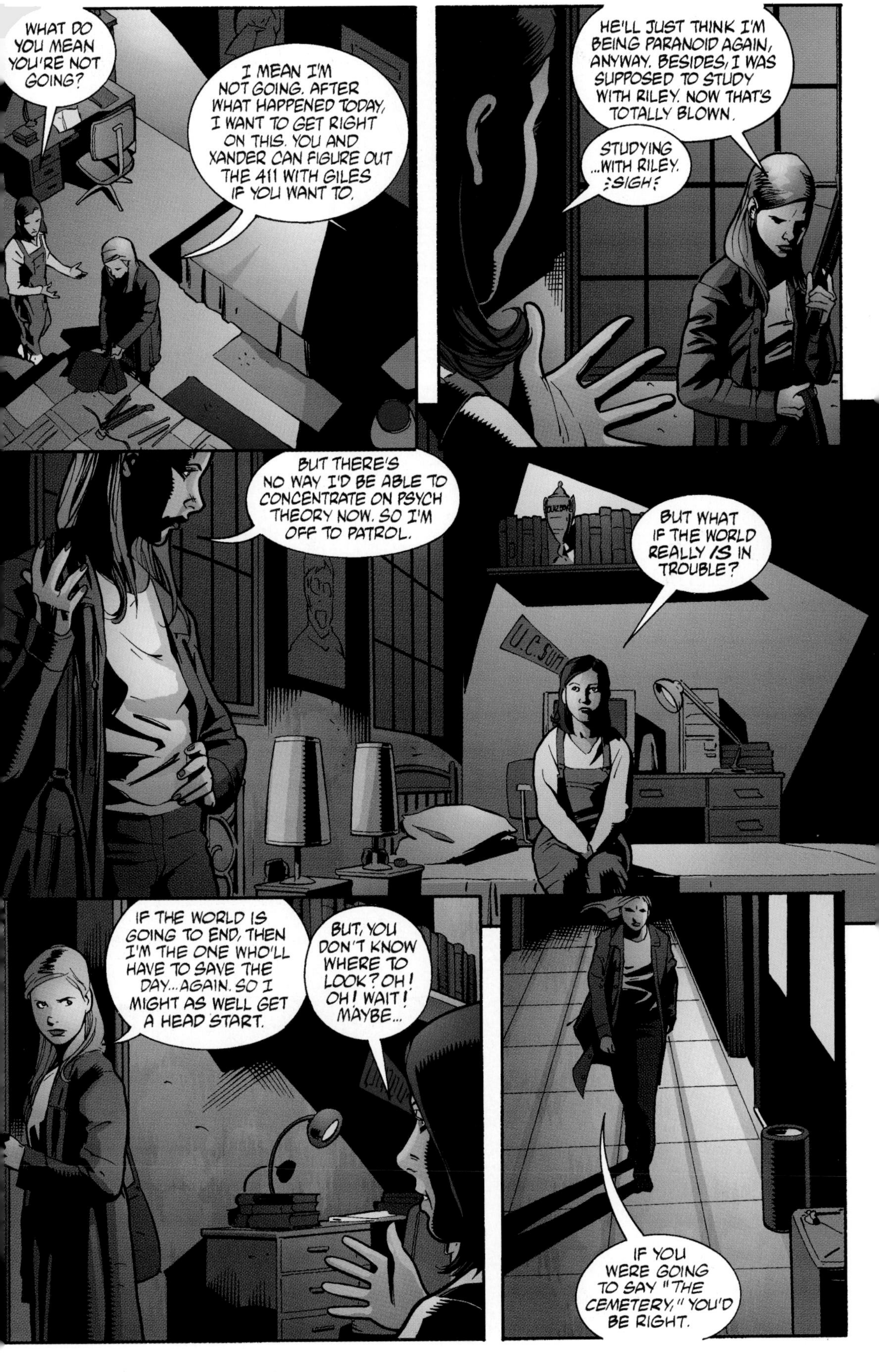
WHAT DO YOU MEAN YOU'RE NOT GOING?
I MEAN I'M NOT GOING. AFTER WHAT HAPPENED TODAY, I WANT TO GET RIGHT ON THIS. YOU AND XANDER CAN FIGURE OUT THE 411 WITH GILES IF YOU WANT TO.
HE'LL JUST THINK I'M BEING PARANOID AGAIN, ANYWAY. BESIDES, I WAS SUPPOSED TO STUDY WITH RILEY. NOW THAT'S TOTALLY BLOWN.
STUDYING ...WITH RILEY. :SIGH:
BUT THERE'S NO WAY I'D BE ABLE TO CONCENTRATE ON PSYCH THEORY NOW. SO I'M OFF TO PATROL.
BUT WHAT IF THE WORLD REALLY IS IN TROUBLE?
IF THE WORLD IS GOING TO END, THEN I'M THE ONE WHO'LL HAVE TO SAVE THE DAY...AGAIN. SO I MIGHT AS WELL GET A HEAD START.
BUT, YOU DON'T KNOW WHERE TO LOOK? OH! OH! WAIT! MAYBE...
IF YOU WERE GOING TO SAY "THE CEMETERY," YOU'D BE RIGHT.

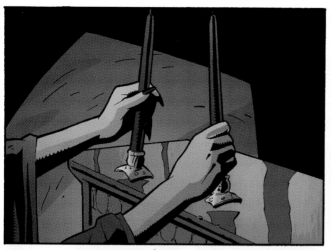

...NOW YOU KNOW AS MUCH AS WE DO.

A CONUNDRUM INDEED.

SO WHAT DO WE DO?

EVERYONE GRAB A BOOK. WE'VE GOT A LOT OF WORK TO DO.

HOW DID I KNOW YOU WERE GOING TO SAY THAT?

RUSTLE
RUSTLE

GREAT, NOW THE CATS ARE GOING ALL WES CRAVEN.

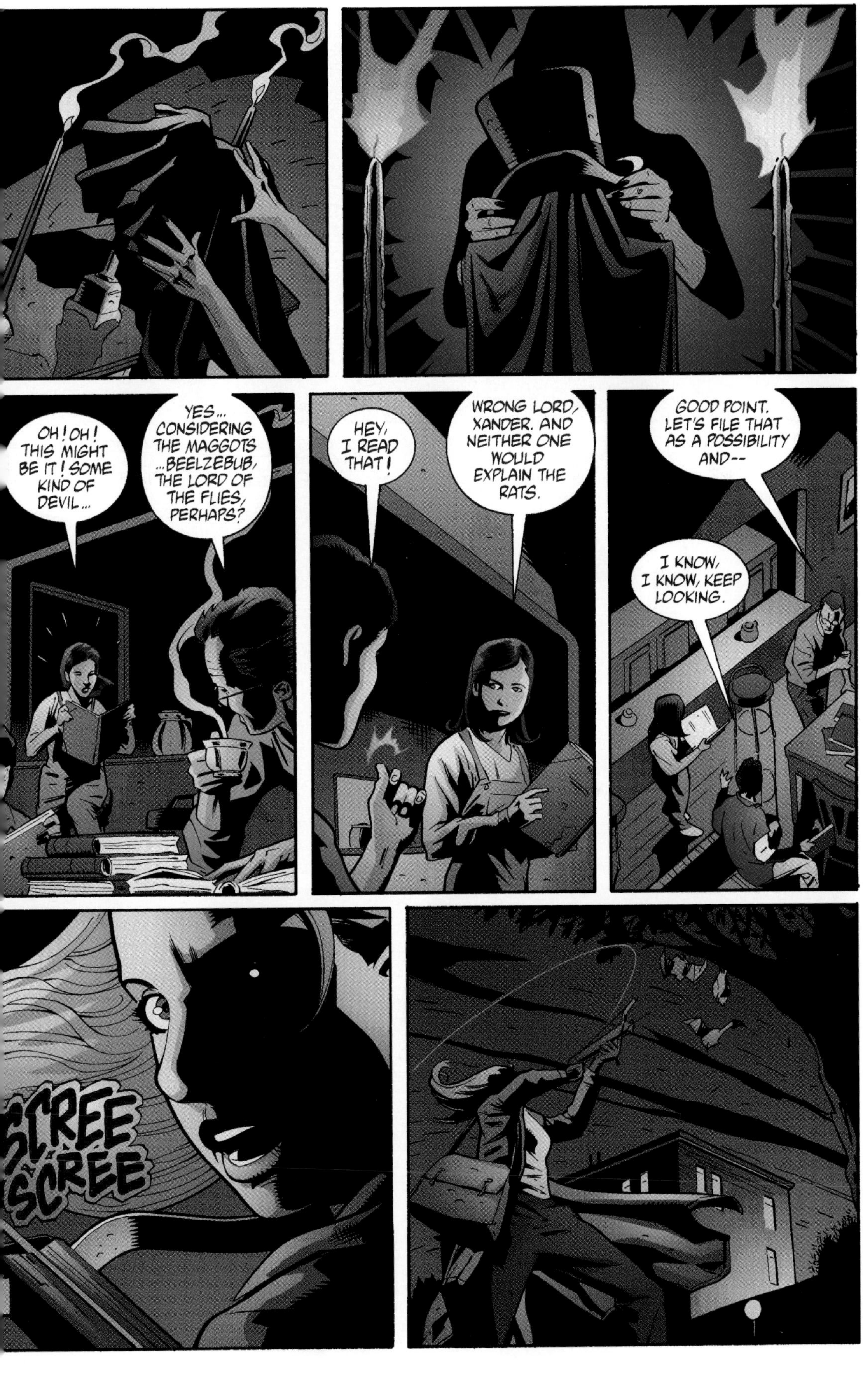
OH! OH! THIS MIGHT BE IT! SOME KIND OF DEVIL...
YES... CONSIDERING THE MAGGOTS ...BEELZEBUB, THE LORD OF THE FLIES, PERHAPS?
HEY, I READ THAT!
WRONG LORD, XANDER. AND NEITHER ONE WOULD EXPLAIN THE RATS.
GOOD POINT. LET'S FILE THAT AS A POSSIBILITY AND--
I KNOW, I KNOW, KEEP LOOKING.
SCREE
SCREE

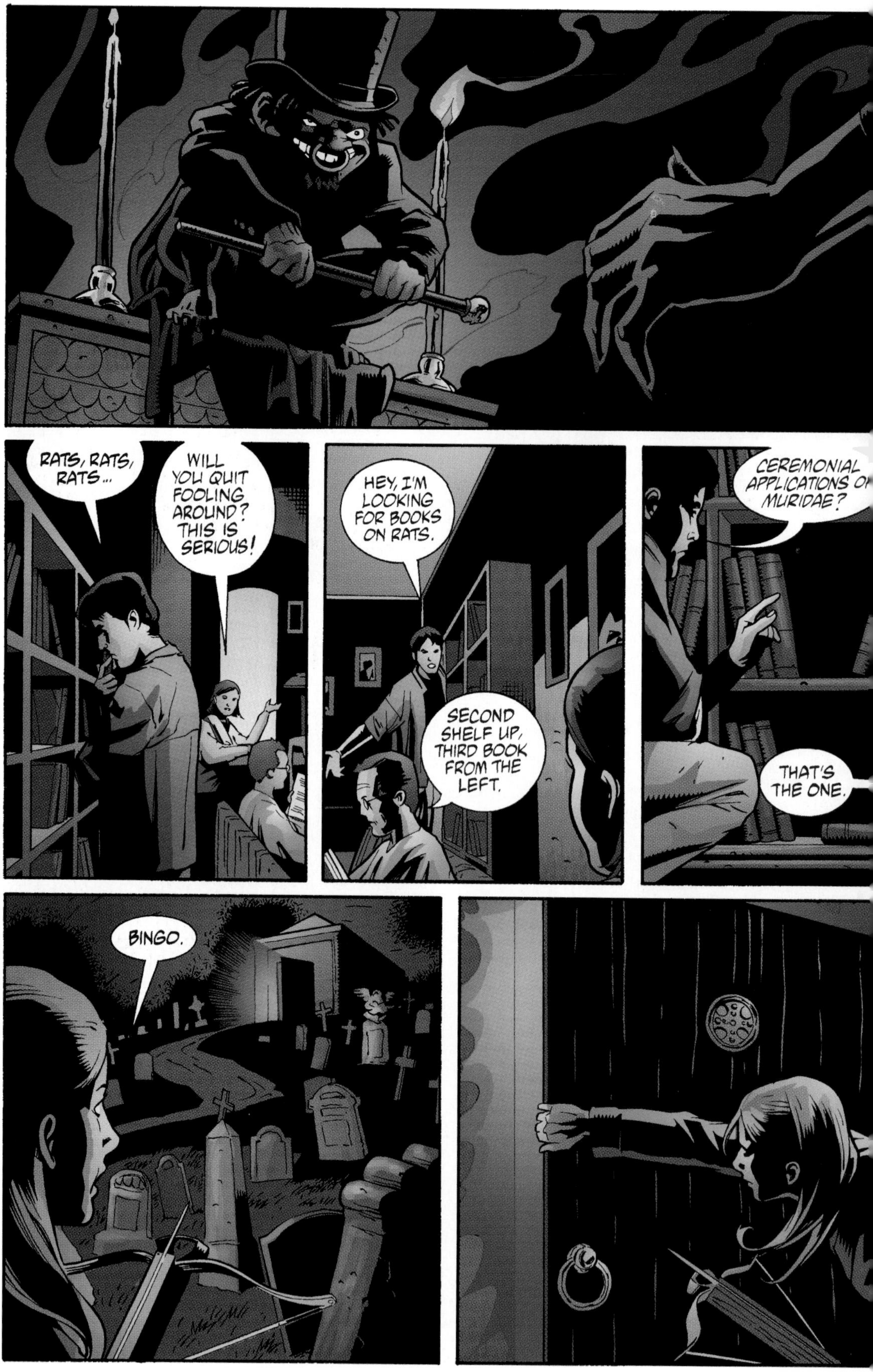
RATS, RATS, RATS...
WILL YOU QUIT FOOLING AROUND? THIS IS SERIOUS!
HEY, I'M LOOKING FOR BOOKS ON RATS.
SECOND SHELF UP, THIRD BOOK FROM THE LEFT.
CEREMONIAL APPLICATIONS OF MURIDAE?
THAT'S THE ONE.
BINGO.

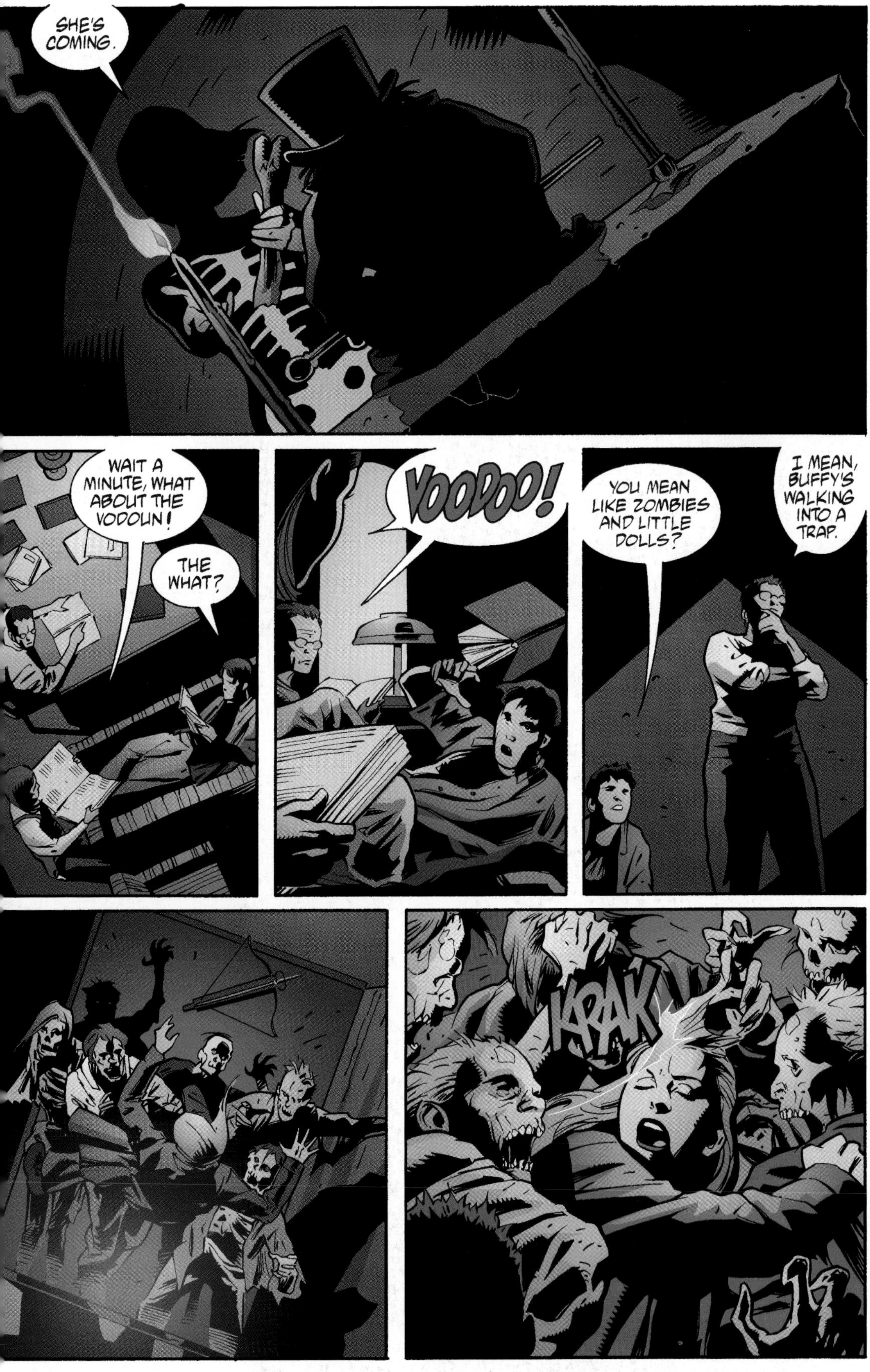

SHE'S COMING.
WAIT A MINUTE, WHAT ABOUT THE VODOUN!
THE WHAT?
VOODOO!
YOU MEAN LIKE ZOMBIES AND LITTLE DOLLS?
I MEAN, BUFFY'S WALKING INTO A TRAP.
KRAK

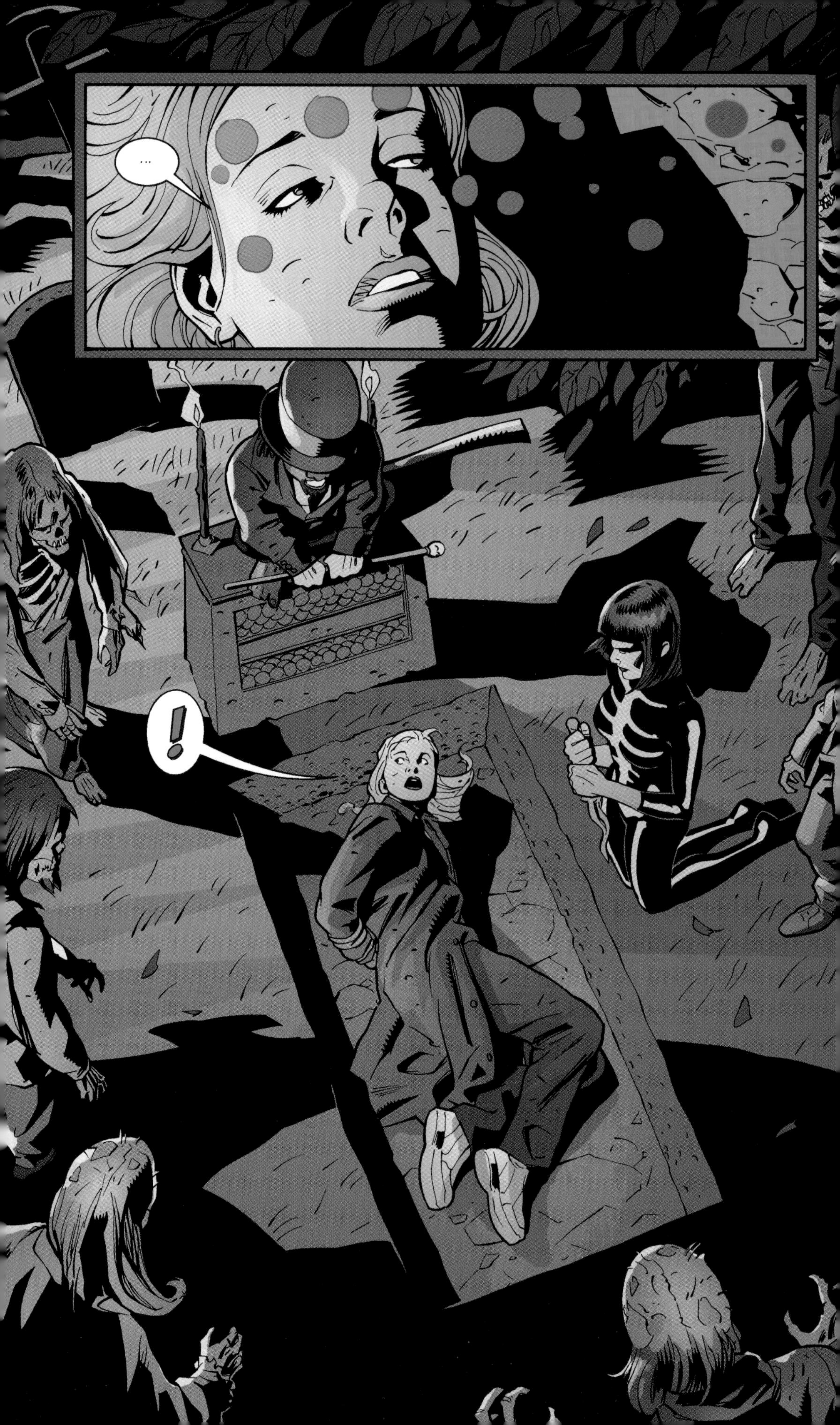
...
!

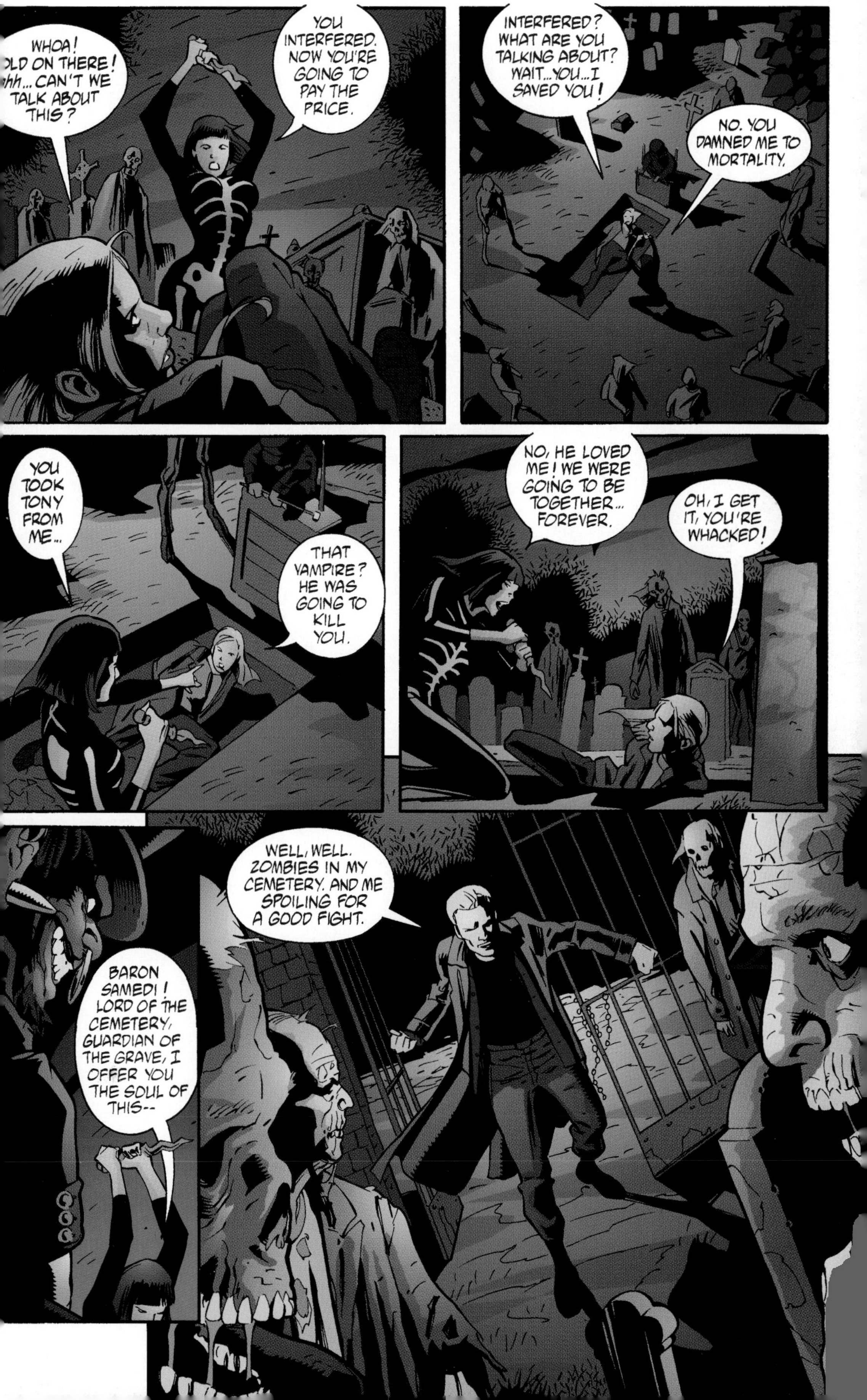
WHOA! OLD ON THERE! hh... CAN'T WE TALK ABOUT THIS?
YOU INTERFERED. NOW YOU'RE GOING TO PAY THE PRICE.
INTERFERED? WHAT ARE YOU TALKING ABOUT? WAIT... YOU... I SAVED YOU!
NO. YOU DAMNED ME TO MORTALITY.
YOU TOOK TONY FROM ME...
THAT VAMPIRE? HE WAS GOING TO KILL YOU.
NO, HE LOVED ME! WE WERE GOING TO BE TOGETHER... FOREVER.
OH, I GET IT, YOU'RE WHACKED!
BARON SAMEDI! LORD OF THE CEMETERY, GUARDIAN OF THE GRAVE, I OFFER YOU THE SOUL OF THIS--
WELL, WELL. ZOMBIES IN MY CEMETERY. AND ME SPOILING FOR A GOOD FIGHT.

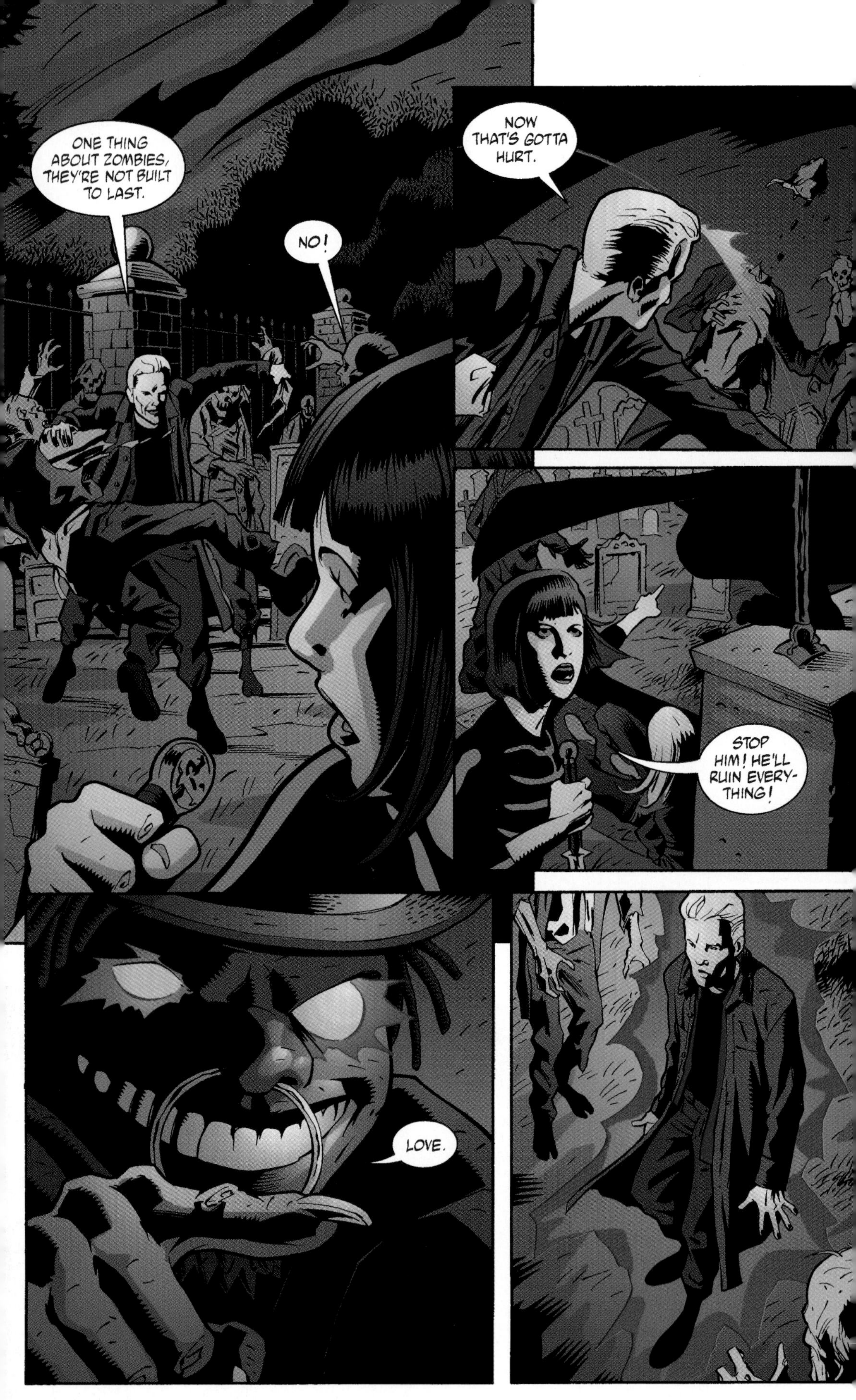
ONE THING ABOUT ZOMBIES, THEY'RE NOT BUILT TO LAST.
NO!
NOW THAT'S GOTTA HURT.
STOP HIM! HE'LL RUIN EVERY-THING!
LOVE.

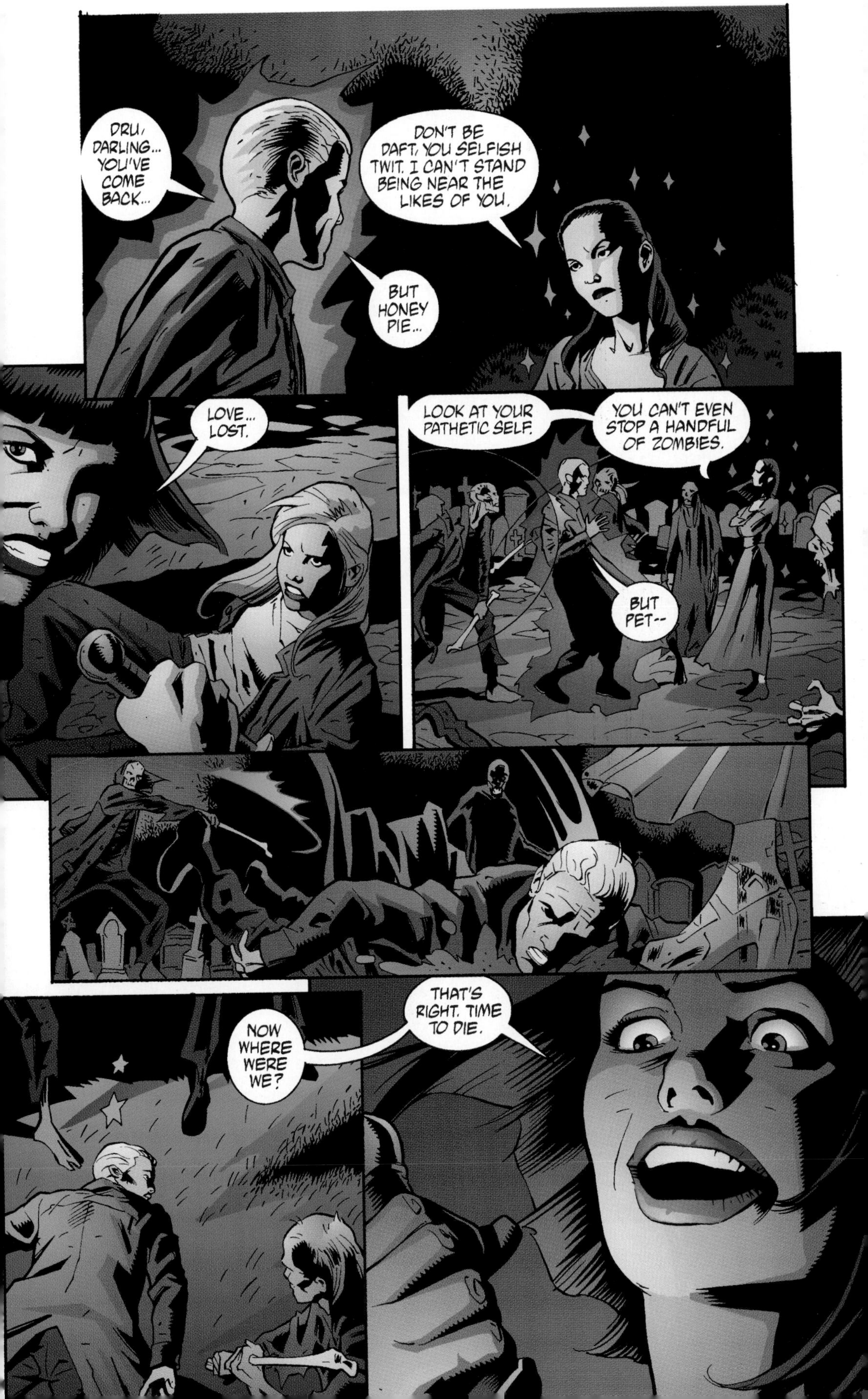
DRU, DARLING... YOU'VE COME BACK...
DON'T BE DAFT, YOU SELFISH TWIT. I CAN'T STAND BEING NEAR THE LIKES OF YOU.
BUT HONEY PIE...
LOVE... LOST.
LOOK AT YOUR PATHETIC SELF.
YOU CAN'T EVEN STOP A HANDFUL OF ZOMBIES.
BUT PET--
NOW WHERE WERE WE?
THAT'S RIGHT. TIME TO DIE.

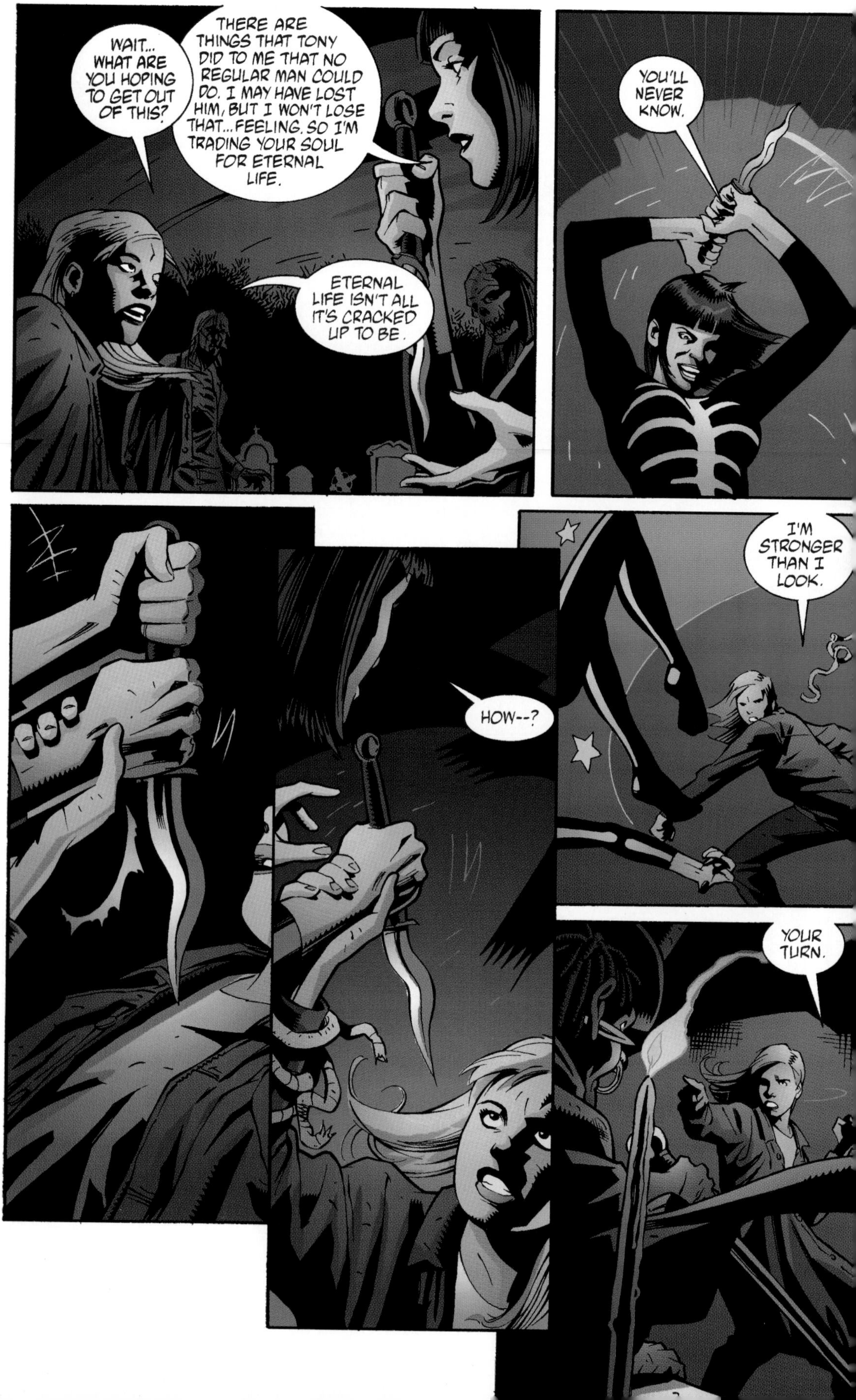

WAIT... WHAT ARE YOU HOPING TO GET OUT OF THIS?
THERE ARE THINGS THAT TONY DID TO ME THAT NO REGULAR MAN COULD DO. I MAY HAVE LOST HIM, BUT I WON'T LOSE THAT...FEELING. SO I'M TRADING YOUR SOUL FOR ETERNAL LIFE.
ETERNAL LIFE ISN'T ALL IT'S CRACKED UP TO BE.
YOU'LL NEVER KNOW.
HOW--?
I'M STRONGER THAN I LOOK.
YOUR TURN.

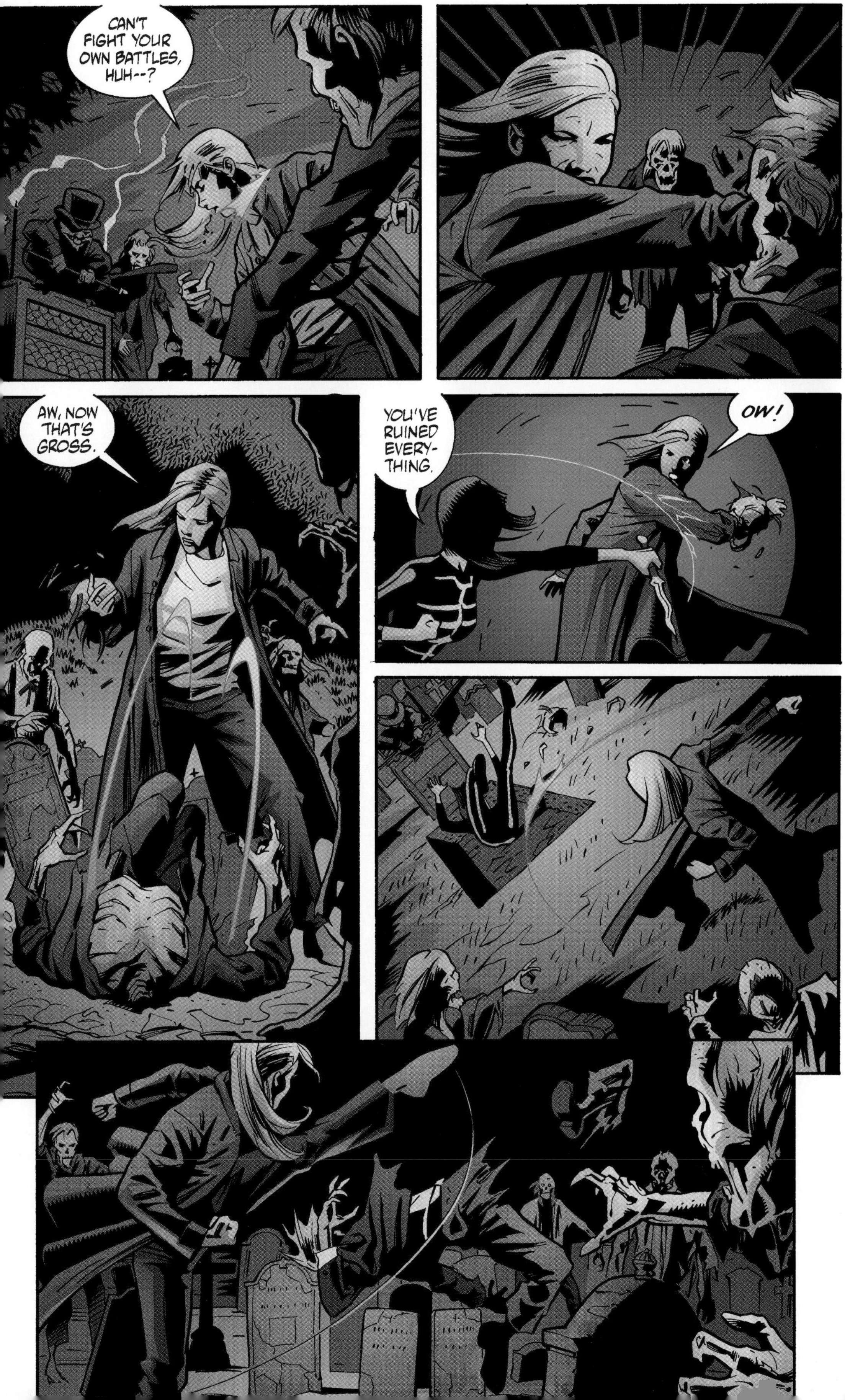
CAN'T FIGHT YOUR OWN BATTLES, HUH--?
AW, NOW THAT'S GROSS.
YOU'VE RUINED EVERY-THING.
OW!

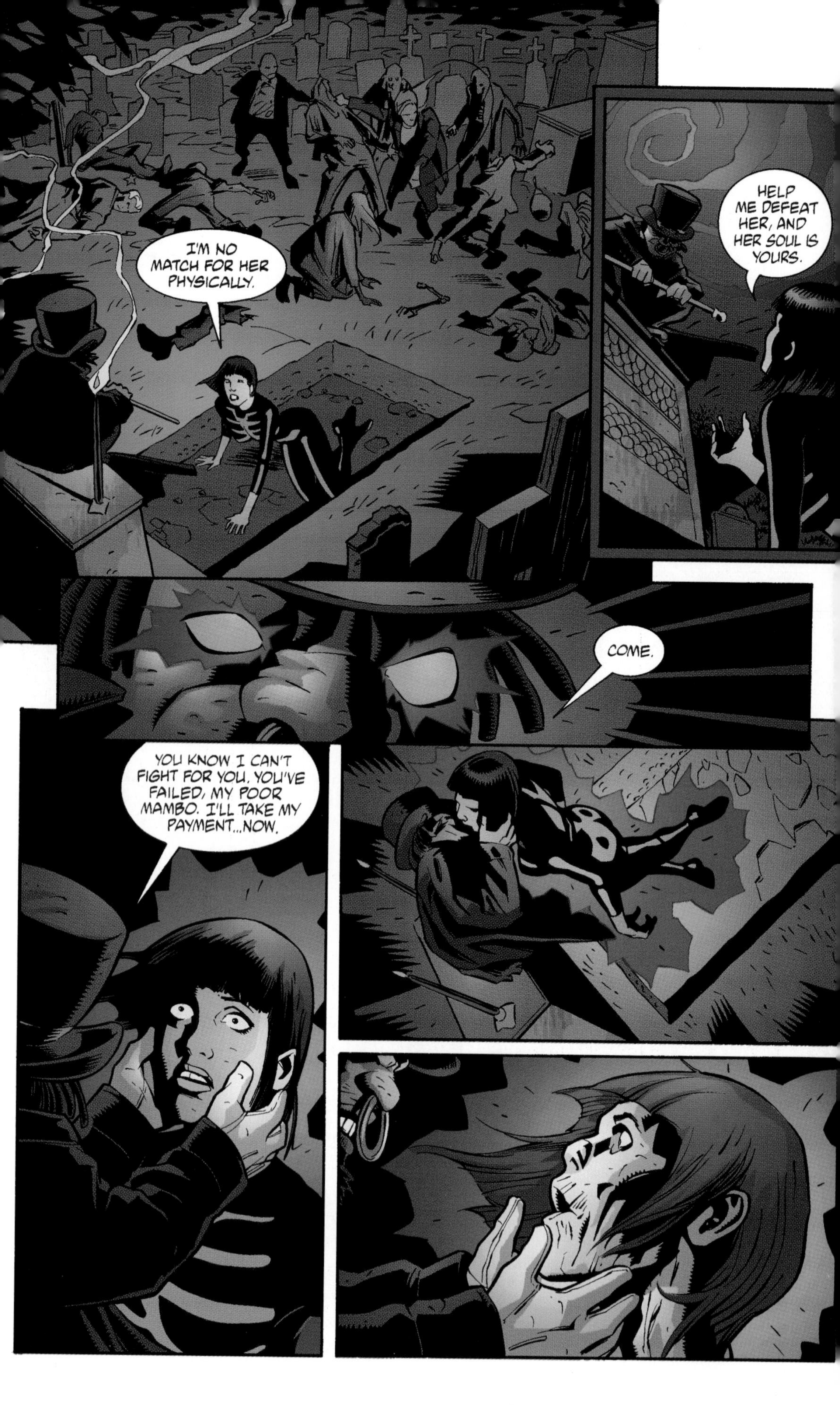
I'M NO MATCH FOR HER PHYSICALLY.
HELP ME DEFEAT HER, AND HER SOUL IS YOURS.
COME.
YOU KNOW I CAN'T FIGHT FOR YOU. YOU'VE FAILED, MY POOR MAMBO. I'LL TAKE MY PAYMENT...NOW.

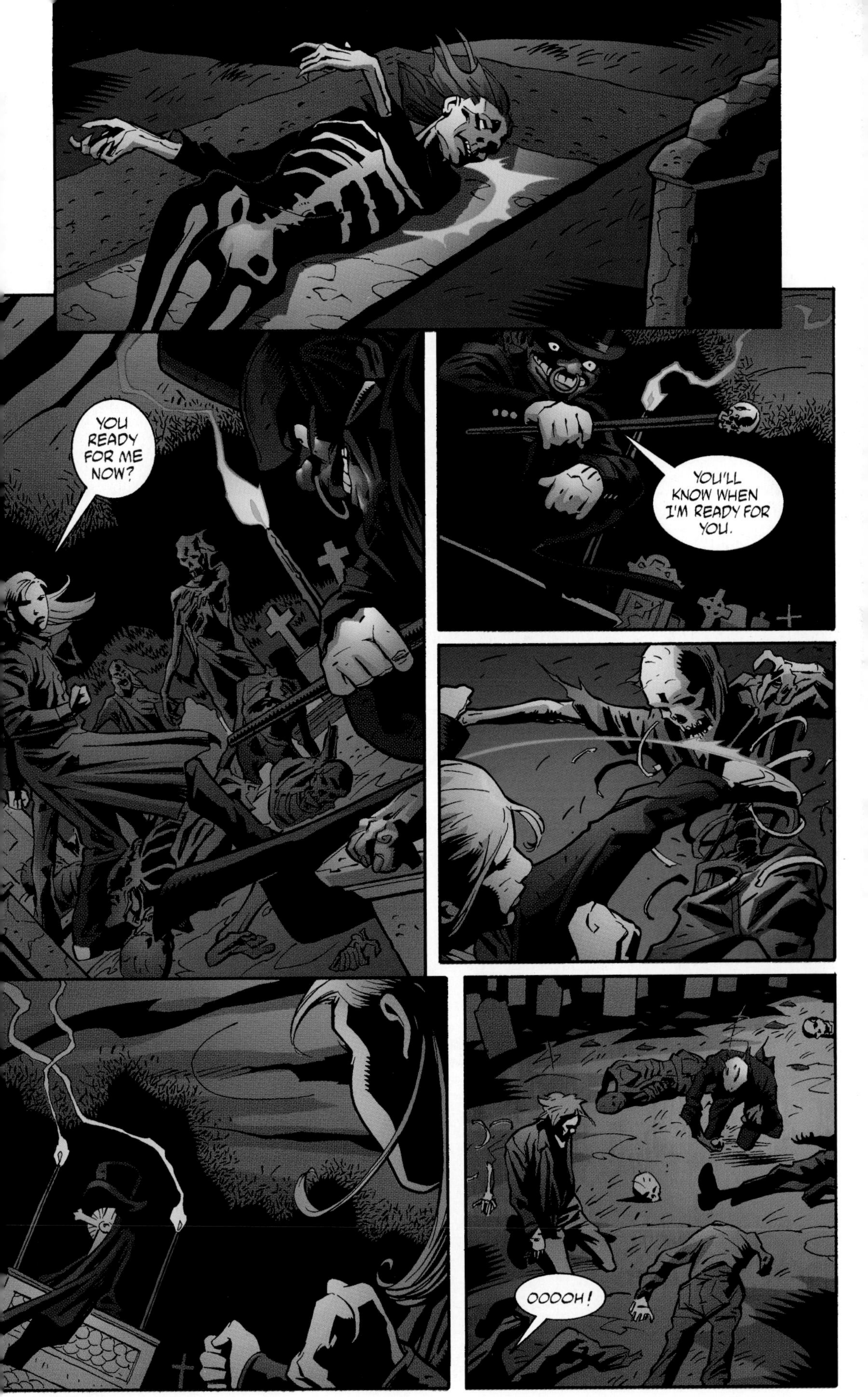
YOU READY FOR ME NOW?
YOU'LL KNOW WHEN I'M READY FOR YOU.
OOOOH!

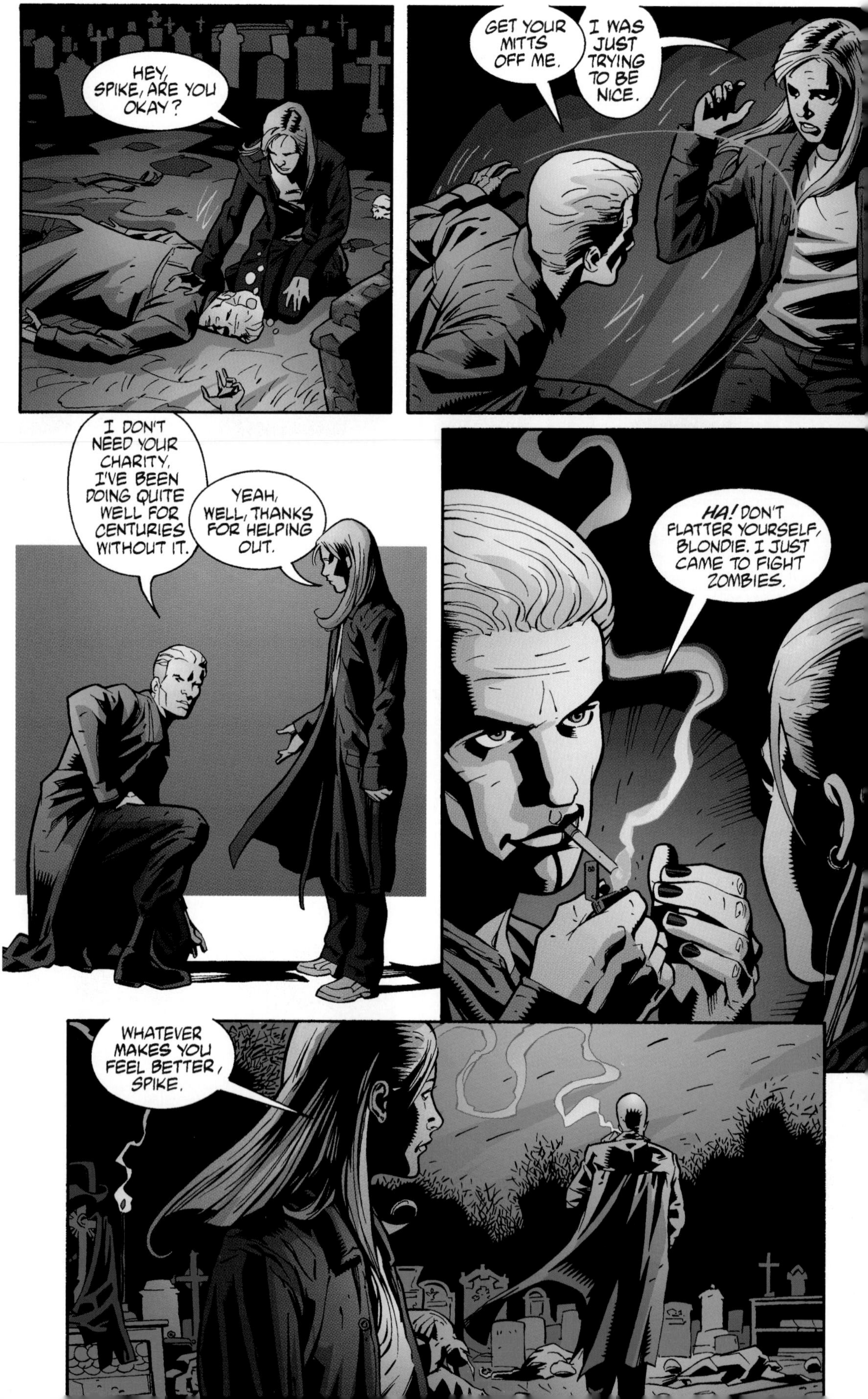
HEY, SPIKE, ARE YOU OKAY?
GET YOUR MITTS OFF ME.
I WAS JUST TRYING TO BE NICE.
I DON'T NEED YOUR CHARITY, I'VE BEEN DOING QUITE WELL FOR CENTURIES WITHOUT IT.
YEAH, WELL, THANKS FOR HELPING OUT.
HA! DON'T FLATTER YOURSELF, BLONDIE. I JUST CAME TO FIGHT ZOMBIES.
WHATEVER MAKES YOU FEEL BETTER, SPIKE.

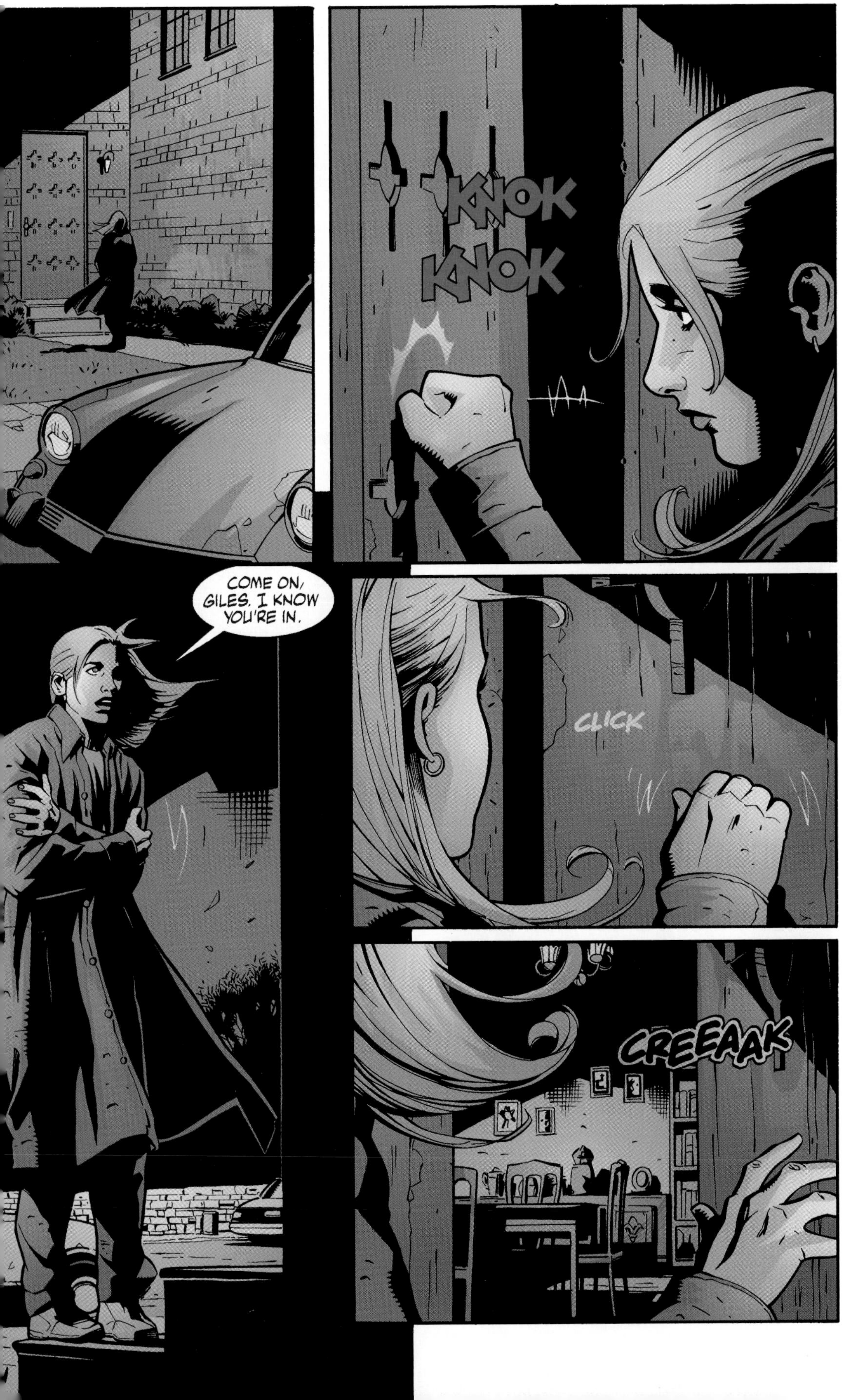
KNOK
KNOK
COME ON, GILES. I KNOW YOU'RE IN.
CLICK
CREEAAK

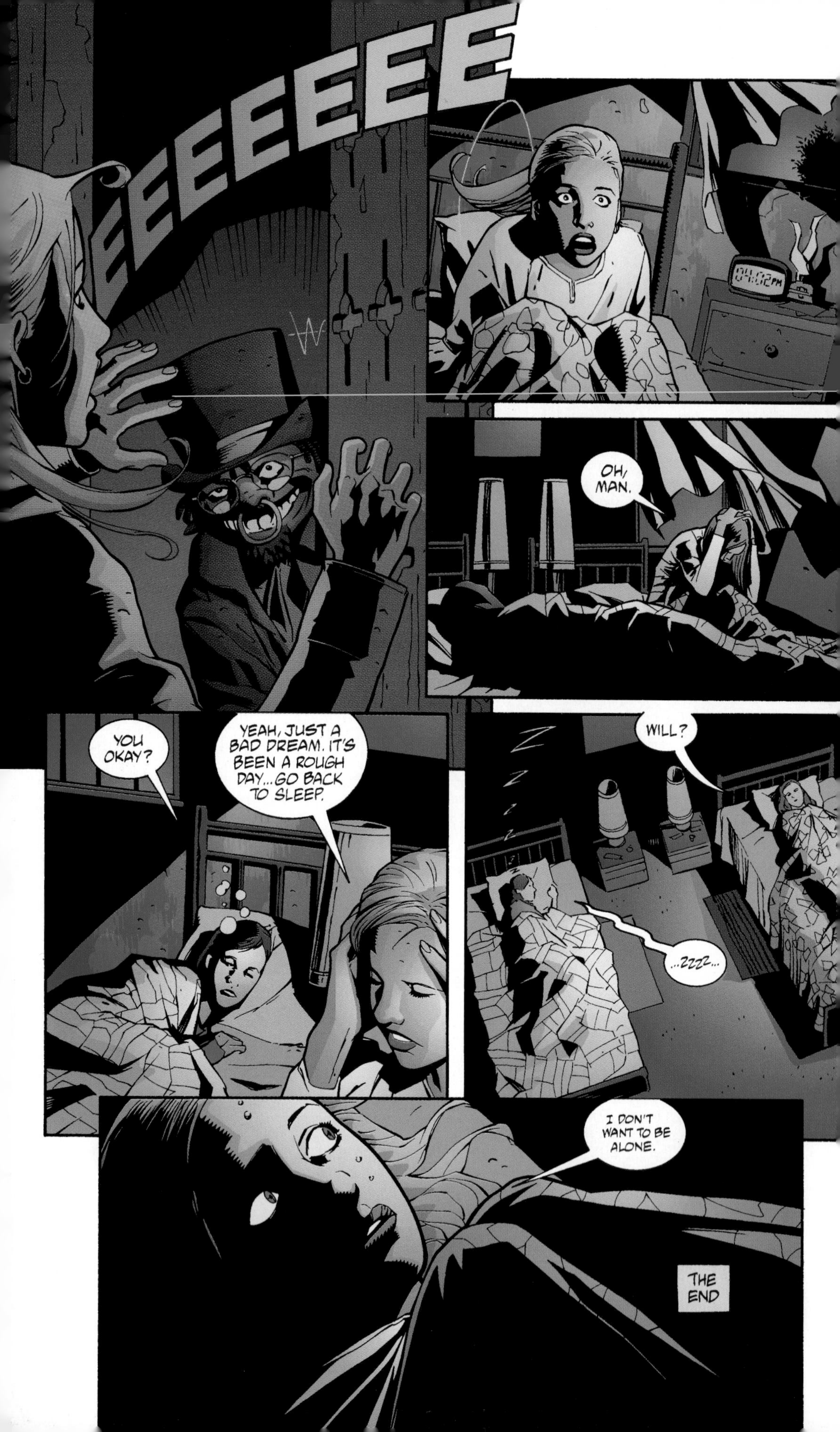
EEEEEEEEE
OH, MAN.
YOU OKAY?
YEAH, JUST A BAD DREAM. IT'S BEEN A ROUGH DAY...GO BACK TO SLEEP.
Z Z Z Z
WILL?
...ZZZZ...
I DON'T WANT TO BE ALONE.
THE END

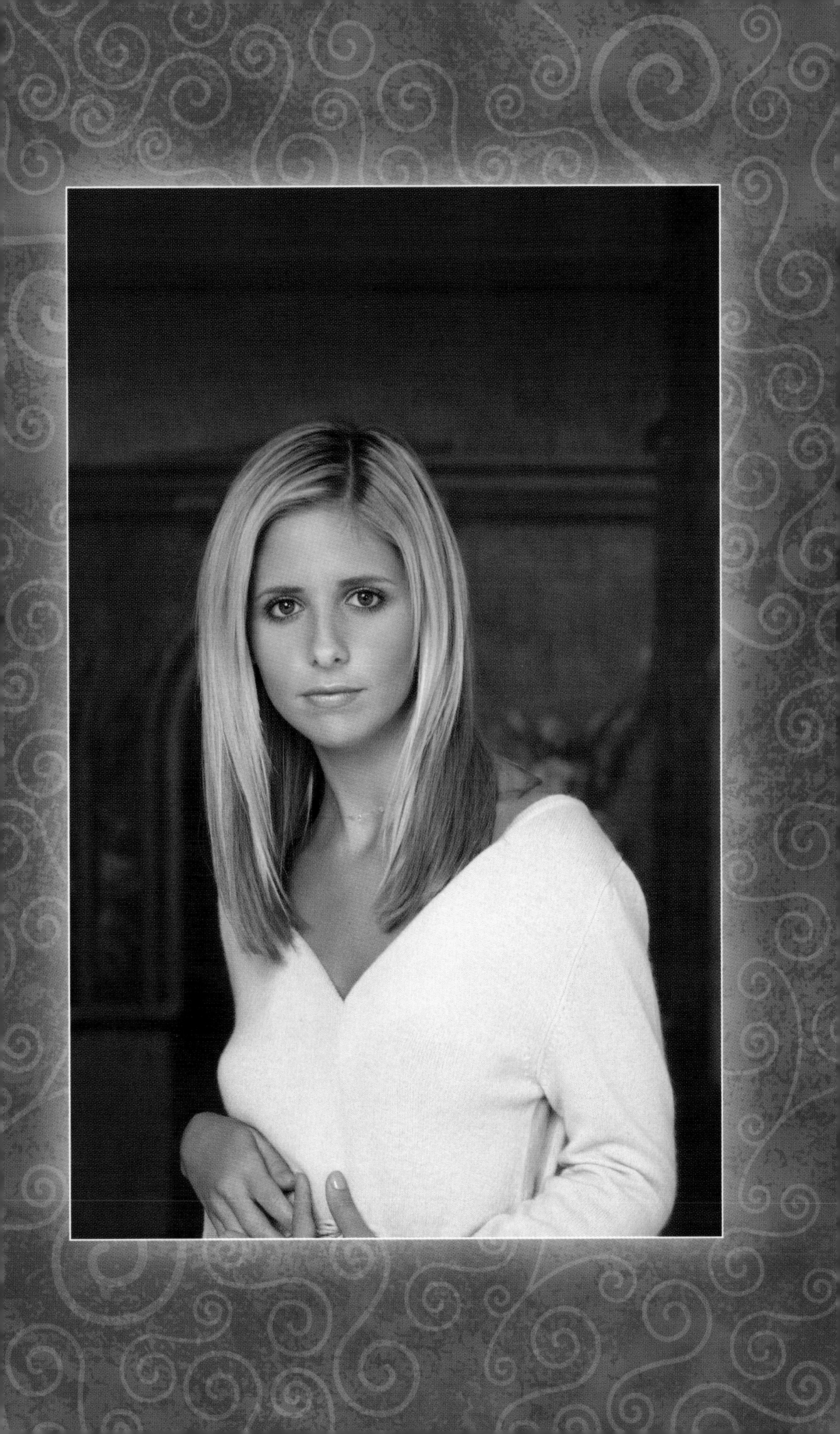

Stake out these Buffy the Vampire Slayer and Angel trade paperbacks

Buffy
the
Vampire Slayer
the

Buffy
the
Vampire Slayer
the
Remaining
Sunlight

Buffy
the
Vampire Slayer
the Origin

Buffy
the
Vampire Slayer
Uninvited Guests

Buffy
the
Vampire Slayer
Ring of Fire

Buffy
Bad Blood

Buffy
the
Crash Test
Demons

Buffy
the
Vampire Slayer
Supernatural Defense Kit

Buffy
the
Vampire Slayer
Pale Reflections

ANGEL
The Hollower
Buffy

ANGEL
Surrogates

ANGEL
Earthly Possessions

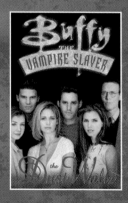

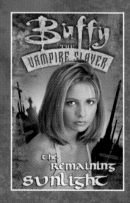

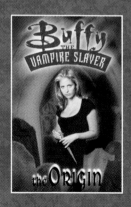

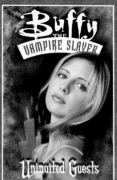

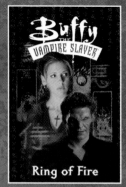

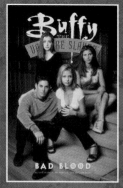

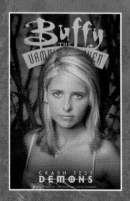

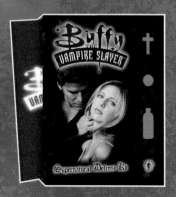

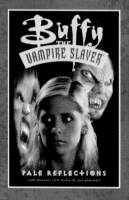

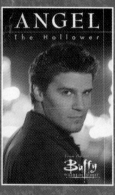

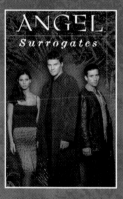

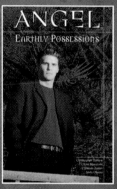

BUFFY THE VAMPIRE SLAYER™, ANGEL™, ALIENS™, AND PREDATOR™ TRADE PAPERBACKS AVAILABLE FROM DARK HORSE COMICS

BUFFY THE VAMPIRE SLAYER

THE DUST WALTZ
Brereton • Gomez • Florea
color paperback
ISBN: 1-56971-342-1 $9.95

THE REMAINING SUNLIGHT
Watson • Bennett • Ketcham
color paperback
ISBN: 1-56971-354-5 $9.95

THE ORIGIN
Golden • Brereton • Bennett • Ketcham
color paperback
ISBN: 1-56971-429-0 $9.95

UNINVITED GUESTS
Watson • Gomez • Florea
color paperback
ISBN: 1-56971-436-3 $10.95

SUPERNATURAL DEFENSE KIT
Watson • Richards • Pimentel
color hardcover w/slipcase
comes with golden-colored cross, "claddagh" ring, and vial of "holy water"
ISBN: 1-56971-486-X $19.95

BAD BLOOD
Watson • Bennett • Ketcham
color paperback
ISBN: 1-56971-445-2 $9.95

CRASH TEST DEMONS
Watson • Richards • Pimentel
color paperback
ISBN: 1-56971-461-4 $9.95

RING OF FIRE
Petrie • Sook
color paperback
ISBN: 1-56971-482-7 $9.95

PALE REFLECTIONS
Watson • Richards • Pimentel
color paperback
ISBN: 1-56971-475-4 $9.95

THE BLOOD OF CARTHAGE
Golden • Richards • Pimentel
color paperback
ISBN: 1-56971-534-3 $12.95

ANGEL

THE HOLLOWER
Golden • Gomez • Florea
color paperback
ISBN: 1-56971-450-9 $9.95

SURROGATES
Golden • Zanier • Owens
color paperback
ISBN: 1-56971-491-6 $9.95

EARTHLY POSSESSIONS
Golden • Sneigoski • Zanier • Owens
color paperback
ISBN: 1-56971-533-5 $9.95

ALIENS

OUTBREAK
Verheiden • Nelson
color paperback
ISBN: 1-56971-174-7 $17.95

NIGHTMARE ASYLUM
Verheiden • Beauvais
color paperback
ISBN: 1-56971-217-4 $16.95

FEMALE WAR
Verheiden • Kieth
color paperback
ISBN: 1-56971-190-9 $16.95

GENOCIDE
Arcudi • Willis • Story
color paperback
ISBN: 1-56971-196-8 $16.95

HARVEST
Prosser • Jones
color paperback
ISBN: 1-56971-198-4 $16.95

ROGUE
Edginton • Simpson
color paperback
ISBN: 1-56971-267-0 $16.95

LABYRINTH
Woodring • Plunkett
color paperback
ISBN: 1-56971-245-X $17.95

STRONGHOLD
Arcudi • Mahnke • Palmiotti
color paperback
ISBN: 1-56971-262-X $16.95

TRIBES
Bissette • Dorman
color hardcover
ISBN: 1-878574-28-0 $24.95

KIDNAPPED
Woodring • Green • Lopez
color paperback
ISBN: 1-56971-372-3 $9.95

APOCALYPSE — THE DESTROYING ANGELS
Schultz • Wheatley
color paperback
ISBN: 1-56971-399-5 $10.95

ALIENS VS PREDATOR

ALIENS VS PREDATOR
Stradley • Norwood • Warner
color paperback
ISBN: 1-56971-125-9 $19.95

THE DEADLIEST OF THE SPECIES
Claremont • Barreto • Guice
color limited hardcover
ISBN: 1-56971-182-8 $99.95

WAR
Stradley • Saltares • Warner
color paperback
ISBN: 1-56971-158-5 $19.95

ETERNAL
Edginton • Maleev
color paperback
ISBN: 1-56971-409-6 $9.95

BATMAN/ALIENS
Marz • Wrightson
color paperback
ISBN: 1-56971-305-7 $14.95

SUPERMAN VS ALIENS
Jurgens • Nowlan
color paperback
ISBN: 1-56971-167-4 $14.95

PREDATOR

CONCRETE JUNGLE
Verheiden • Warner • Randall
color paperback
ISBN: 1-56971-165-8 $14.95

BIG GAME
Arcudi • Dorkin • Gil
color paperback
ISBN: 1-56971-166-6 $14.95

COLD WAR
Verheiden • Randall • Mitchell
color paperback
ISBN: 1-878574-79-5 $13.95

RACE WAR
Vachss • Stradley • Raskin • Pelle
color paperback
ISBN: 1-56971-112-7 $17.95

HELL & HOT WATER
Schultz • Colan
color paperback
ISBN: 1-56971-271-9 $9.95

KINDRED
Lamb • Tolson • O'Connell • Peterson
color paperback
ISBN: 1-56971-270-0 $14.95

PREDATOR VS JUDGE DREDD
Wagner • Alcatena
color paperback
ISBN: 1-56971-345-6 $9.95

TARZAN VS PRED[illegible]R AT THE EARTH'S C[illegible]
Simonson • Weeks
color paperback
ISBN: 1-56971-231-X $1[illegible]

Available from your local comics shop or bookstore!

To find a comics shop in your area, call 1-888-266-4226
For more information or to order direct:
•On the web: www.darkhorse.com •E-mail: mailorder@darkhorse.com
•Phone: 1-800-862-0052 or (503) 652-9701 Mon.-Sat. 9 A.M. to 5 P.M. Pacific Time
*Prices and availability subject to change without notice

Dark Horse Comics: **Mike Richardson** *publisher* • **Neil Hankerson** *executive vi[illegible] president* • **Andy Karabatsos** *vice president of finance* • **Randy Stradley** *vice president [illegible]ishing* • **Chris [illegible]rner** *senior editor* • **Michael Martens** *vice president of marketing* • **Anita Nelson** *vice president of sales & li[illegible]g* • **David Scroggy** *vice president of product development* • **Mark Cox** *art director* • **Dale LaFountain** *vice pres[illegible]f information technology* • **Kim Haines** *director of human resources* • **Darlene Vogel** *director of purchasing* • [illegible]izzi • *general counsel*